Disney
GRAVITY FALLS

Dipper's and Mabel's Guide to Mystery and Nonstop Fun!

written by Dipper Pines and Mabel Pines

With help from Rob Renzetti, Shane Houghton, and Stephanie Ramirez
Additional help by Dipper and Mabel's assistant, Eric Geron ← our editor!

Based on the series created by Alex Hirsch

Disney PRESS
Los Angeles • New York

THIS BOOK IS PROPERTY OF

_____

BLAH BLAH BLAH

Copyright © 2014 Disney Enterprises, Inc.

Printed in the United States of America
First Edition
5 7 9 11 10 8 6 4
G475-5664-5-15153
ISBN 978-1-4847-1080-7
Library of Congress Control Number: 2014941799

I'm a congressman!

I think this might be a code. More on codes later.

For more Disney Press fun, visit www.disneybooks.com
Visit DisneyXD.com

To whatever intrepid mystery hunter gets their hands on this book, my name is Dipper Pines. During my summer in the strange town of Gravity Falls, I've seen so many paranormal and baffling things that I could fill up an entire book! Lucky for me (and for you) I found this (cursed?) empty old book up in the attic of the Mystery Shack. By the time I'm done writing and you're done reading, you'll have all you need to know to become a world-class Paranormal Expert like myself. In addition, if I'm kidnapped, blasted into another dimension, turned to stone, or taken by forces I can't imagine—I may call on you to save me one day—so take notes!   ——Dipper

LOL!

Hey there! Mabel Pines here!
I had to jump on Dipper's bed for a full half hour before he agreed to let me coauthor his book. And lucky for you, the fun factor of this little project just skyrocketed 1,010 percent!!!! If you read my sections (and why wouldn't you?), you'll learn everything you need to know to become the funnest kid in your neighborhood, your town, and maybe—just maybe—the whole world!!!!!!

♡ Mabel

I apologize in advance for my
sister's ~~participation~~ fart in this book.

3

About the Author

Dipper Pines currently resides in Gravity Falls, Oregon, where he solves mysteries and keeps the forces of ~~darkness~~ DORKNESS at bay. "The Legend of the Gobblewonker" and "The Curious Case of the Beheaded Waxman" are among his legendary adventures, which you can read about in the Home and Garden section of the *Gravity Falls Gossiper*. He has been awarded the distinguished President's Key and had his bedtime pushed back from nine to ten-thirty in recognition of his achievements.

← THIS GUY!

About the COOLER Author

Mabel Pines is qualified to write about fun because she is the most fun person in the world! As evidence, I'm not going to make you read a big long bio like some people . . . but instead, here's a drawing of a cute cat balancing on a giant strawberry! Or maybe it's a tiny cat on a regular-sized strawberry. You decide!

DON'T LICK THIS CHOCOLATE STAIN! I'M SAVING IT FOR LATER.

Your Guide to This Guide

WHEEEE!!

MABEL'S GUIDE
to
the FUN Stuff

Forget about all those silly titles and numbers! If you want to get to the fun stuff, just look for Mabel's Seal of Quality! When you see one of these, you know you're in for a good time with some:

MABEL'S SEAL of QUALITY

FUN ACTIVITIES!

FUN CRAFT PROJECTS!

FUN CHALLENGES!

SERIOUS INSIGHTS INTO THE MYSTERIES OF LIFE!

JUST KIDDING! (THAT'S ONE OF MABEL'S FUN JOKES!)

Gotta keep it light with Dipper doling out all the gloom and doom!

WATCH OUT FOR MYSTERY!

Fun with Allies and Enemies

Before you begin your investigation, you have to learn to distinguish friend from foe. Sometimes the scariest creatures you'll encounter are the normal people you meet! And I'm not just talking about my Grunkle Stan first thing in the morning. (Although I wish I could get that image out of my head.)

Here is a list of some of my allies and enemies, in case you ever encounter them yourself!

Grunkle Stan

Distinguishing Feature:
Mysterious fez/absurd amounts of shoulder hair

Special Ability:
Can lie in .00531 seconds

Status: Ally

Grunkle Stan has the heart of a lion and the face of a bridge troll!

STAN

Soos

Distinguishing Feature:
Large stomach bones

Special Ability:
Can break/fix anything

Status: Ally

Soos

Soos is like a giant anime panda creature that makes the forests grow and lets you sleep on his tummy.

Wendy

Distinguishing Feature:
Impossibly cool

Special Ability:
Can create origami with an axe

Status: Ally

WENDY

In my mind, Wendy is a WARRIOR PRINCESS from the moons of VENUS!!

9

Lil' Gideon

<u>Distinguishing Feature:</u>
Giant and frightening white hair

<u>Special Ability:</u>
An admittedly beautiful singing voice

<u>Status:</u> Enemy

Yuck!

Bleeachh!!

BOOOOOO!!!!!!

Robbie

<u>Distinguishing Feature:</u>
His black hair, black hoodie, and black pants

<u>Special Ability:</u>
Making girls like him for NO REASON WHATSOEVER!

<u>Status:</u>
Enemy? Ally? Frenemy?

He wears more makeup than I do!

Candy

<u>Distinguishing Feature:</u>
Very thick glasses

<u>Special Ability:</u>
an stare at you without blinking for a really, really long time

<u>Status:</u> Mabel's friends are . . . odd

Dipper doesn't appreciate Candy's inner beauty! I've told her she should wear her inner beauty on the outside, but Candy says that her guts would just go spilling out all over.

Grenda

<u>Distinguishing Feature:</u>
That voice!

<u>Special Ability:</u>
I think her entire torso might be one big muscle

<u>Status:</u> I'm calling her an ally because I wouldn't want to get on her bad side. Have you seen those arms?

When I become president, e's gonna be my bodyguard!

Mabel

Distinguishing Feature:
Her endless supply
of homemade sweaters

Special Ability:
Her unique view of life

Status:
My Closest Ally and
Best Friend

Aww! Thanks, Bro-bro!
Here, let me do one
for you!

Dipper

Distinguishing Feature:
That pine tree trucker
hat biz. Also his squeaky
puberty voice!

Special Ability:
Can sneeze like a kitten

Status:
The Best Brother in the
Entire World!! Although h
could stand to shower mo

I may have to change
Mabel's status to "Enemy."

Is Something ~~SUPERNATURAL~~ Fun Going On?

I know, I know. You're saying, "Why would I be reading this book if there wasn't something strange going on?" Well, the mystery of why your sister takes so long in the bathroom may be hard to solve, but that doesn't mean the answer is outside the laws of nature.

Before you can become a master of the paranormal like me, you need to be able to tell the difference between the merely odd and the truly miraculous.

SIGHTS, SOUNDS, and SMELLS to Watch Out For

Out of context, hair, odors, and strange noises are often mistaken for proof of the supernatural. Ask yourself these hard questions before jumping to conclusions:

HAIRBALL—Is this definitive evidence that werewolves are invading your town at night? Or is your sister shedding?

ECTOPLASMIC GOO—Is that puddle of thick liquid physical residue from a paranormal creature? Or did Waddles drool on the floor?

EAR-PIERCING SCREECH—Is that a demon being summoned from the underworld? Or Robbie screaming out one of his original "songs"?

SICKENING STENCH—Does the pungent smell of rotten eggs and motor oil mixed with sewage mean you're being visited by a dumpster troll? Or is Old Man McGucket trying to cook again?

GHASTLY GROAN—Is this the sound of a tortured soul, longing to escape to the ghostly afterlife? Or is your Grunkle Stan trying to get out of his chair?

BURNING ODOR—Can that eye-watering stench of rotting, heated organic waste be an evil fairy attempting a séance? Or did your sister just discover perfume?

Mabel's PUMP UP THE FUN Challenge!

Okay, let's shove all the weirdo stuff aside and turn your humdrum afternoon into a Record-Setting Event! There are opportunities for record setting all around you! You just need to know how to look!! On this very page I am writing, there are challenges to be had!!! For instance, how many exclamation points can you use at the end of a sentence?!!!?!!!!!!!!!?!!! (New record=15.)

OR HOW BIG CAN YOU MAKE THE LETTERS?

Or how many interesting, strange, exciting, crazy, surprising, goofy, startling, bewildering, thrilling, bizarre, outlandish, wild, silly, senseless, ridiculous, zany adjectives can you use in a row?

Or . . . how many times can you write your favorite word on one page? I'll go first. My favorite word (and favorite pet pig) is Waddles.

16

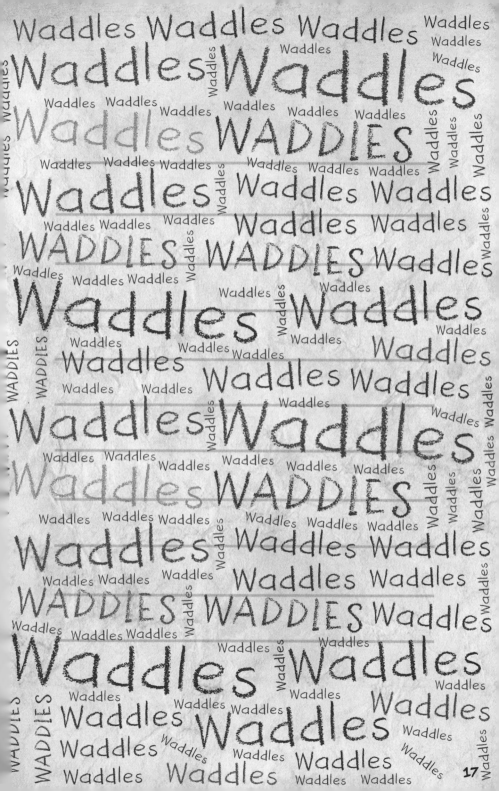

How many times did I write "Waddles"? Do you think you can beat my record? Pick your favorite word (your real favorite, not a short word like "it" or "or") and see how many times you can write it in the space below:

Strange Weather We're Having, or SUPERNATURAL OMEN?

The natural world can come up with some pretty strange stuff all on its own. A paranormal investigator needs to develop a keen sense of which conditions call for an umbrella and which call for hiding in your top secret headquarters. Can you tell which events described below are just weird weather or other astrological events and which are signs of the supernatural?

1) Swirling winds (that lift your house off the ground)
   Natural _____ Supernatural _____

2) Large ice balls (that fall like rain)
   Natural _____ Supernatural _____

3) There are three suns
   Natural _____ Supernatural _____

4) Frogs (that fall from the sky)
   Natural _____ Supernatural _____

5) The moon turns blue
   Natural _____ Supernatural _____

6) Blood rain
   Natural _____ Supernatural _____

7) The sun turns black
   Natural _____ Supernatural _____

Okay, so I gave you some easy ones to start with. But, believe it or not, they are ALL natural events! I'll give you a moment to recompose yourself since **I just BLEW YOUR MIND.**

1) <u>Tornado</u>—They do some strange stuff but twisters are completely natural.

2) <u>Hail</u>—Yes, of course. But did you know that hailstones can get really big? One was 80 pounds!

3) <u>Sun Dogs or Sun Ghosts</u>—When the sun is low in the sky and the right kind of moisture is in the air, it can appear that the sun has a couple of clones. More on real clones later.

4) <u>Nonaqueous Rain</u>—Fish have also been known to fall like rain. The theory is that tornadoes pass over water, suck up the creatures in the water, and then dump them out later. Legit terrifying, huh?

5) <u>Blue Moon</u>—Another trick of light and water in the sky. The moisture mixes with volcanic ash and forest fire soot to change the color of the moon. Other mixes of stuff can turn it orange or red.

6) <u>Blood Rain</u>—Again, this is just junk like sand or dust in the air combining with the rainwater.

7) <u>Solar Eclipse</u>—The black shape is the moon getting between the Earth and the sun. A total eclipse only happens when all three are lined up exactly right and you are in the right location to see it. And then you aren't even supposed to look at it! But our buddy Soos has a way around that problem that he'll explain on the next few pages.

So what are the *actual* signs of the supernatural? It's not always easy to tell, but if you see one of the following, you know something is up:

1) Gravity stops working and everybody floats off the ground.

2) Your pet dog or cat gets up on two legs, starts talking, and wants to take the car to the movies.

3) The water in your swimming pool turns into blood. (Pool party—ruined!)

4) Your books fly off the bookshelf and head south for the winter.

5) The living room carpet turns into quicksand and your sofa is sucked down into the basement.

6) This guy appears:

He says his name is "Bill," and the last time I saw him he said something about "everything changing" in the near future. He can invade your dreams and even take control of a person's body. Watch out for him. He could be hiding anywhere. And whatever you do, do NOT chant his name three times in a darkened room. TRUST ME. **DO NOT SUMMON AT ALL COSTS!**

Soos: Handyman of Mystery—How to Make an Eclipse Viewer

Hey, dudes! Staring into the sun during an eclipse is dangerous and "straight painful," to quote Sev'ral Timez band member Chubby Z. Here's how to make your very own eclipse viewer.

What You'll Need:

A box. (I prefer a cereal box. And I prefer a cereal like Clustery Bunches of Owls.)

A piece of white paper as big as the bottom of the box.

A small bit of tinfoil. If you have some left over, you can make one of those dope tinfoil hats like Old Man McGucket wears.

Sticky stuff. Glue and/or tape.

Pointy stuff. A pin or needle and scissors.

An adult. You don't want to be fooling around with pointy things without someone watching out for you, dude.

What You Do:

Step 1—Eat all the cereal. Very important step. Empties out the box and will make you a champion track runner, according to the commercials.

Step 2—Glue the piece of white paper to the bottom of the cereal box.

Step 3—Cut the ends off the top of the box tabs. Now you got two openings, dawg.

Step 4—Tape the tinfoil over one of the openings.

Step 5—Poke a small hole in the foil with the pin or needle.

Step 6—Hold the viewer with the sun shining down on the pinhole and foil.

Step 7—Look through the other opening and move the box around till you see the sun on the bottom. You're totally owning that eclipse, dude!

Warning! This viewer is for solar eclipses only! Do not attempt to use for a lunar eclipse or its powers will be harnessed for evil. You might turn into a werewolf or something. That's a real thing. My cousin Reggie's seen it happen, dudes.

Mabel's "Insta-Hat"

When weird weather strikes, you may have the urge to fashionably cover your head RIGHT NOW! Don't worry! Mabel's got your back! In a pinch, use one of the following as an "Insta-Hat" (patent pending):

⭐ Sweater Head-Wrap!

Wrap that fluffy puppy around your noggin for flashy fun. However, if you were previously wearing that sweater, be sure to have something on underneath.

⭐ Book Hat!

Take this book you're holding right now, flip it over, and put that sucker on your head! . . . You look so good right now.

⭐ Pet Cap!

Got a pet? Put it on your head! Most animals won't stay on your head for long. (I know from experience.) USE DUCT TAPE!! Or a pretty ribbon with a bow!!!!!

Preparing for Your
SUPERNATURAL Encounter 3

So you've confirmed that something otherworldly is happening. But are you prepared to confront the supernatural? Test your readiness with this quiz:

ARE YOU READY FOR THIS?
A Quiz to See If You Have What It Takes:

1) When I discover a monster living in my refrigerator, I:
A) scream and run. B) scream and cower in place. C) stifle a scream and reach for the ketchup. D) throw the fridge off a cliff and watch it explode on the rocks below.

2) The best tool for combating evil is:
A) a positive outlook! B) something pointy. C) a journal of the supernatural. D) my bare fists.

3) My attitude toward trouble is:
A) to avoid it at all costs. B) to avoid it whenever possible. C) to deal with it when it comes my way. D) trouble better watch out for me.

4) I can best be described as:
A) just a scared kid. B) a normal kid. C) a normal kid who can do special things. D) the best kid for the job.

5) When you are trapped and there is no way out, you think:
A) Aaahhhhh! B) Please, no! No!! C) There's always some way out! D) Whatever's trapped me is in for it now!

SCORING

Give yourself one point for each time you answered **A**, two for **B**, three for **C**, and four for **D**, then total your score.

5–8 Points "Scaredy Scarederson"—Maybe you should stay home. See what's on TV.

9–12 Points "Thompson"—Come with us but hang back a little.

13–16 Points "Investigator Material!"—Sounds like you and me have a lot in common. Want to join our team?

17–20 Points "The Author of Journal #3?"—Wow, you must be a superhero. Why are you even reading this book? I should be learning from you!

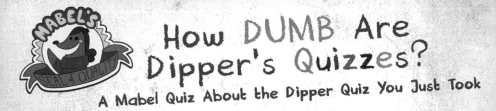

How DUMB Are Dipper's Quizzes?

A Mabel Quiz About the Dipper Quiz You Just Took

1) Dipper asks about your scream, but Dipper's scream:
   A) sounds like a nine-year-old girl. B) sounds like a three-year-old girl. C) sounds like a dolphin caught in a net. D) can only be heard by dogs.

2) The best tool for answering Dipper's quiz is:
   A) a skeptical attitude. B) something pointy, like a pencil. C) tricking him into answering it for you. D) feeding it to the goat.

3) My attitude toward question three is:
   A) it should have been question one. B) three questions is already too many. C) to answer it when it comes my way. D) three is a magic number. So watch out for its magic powers!

4) I can best describe Dipper's quiz as:
   A) something dumb for dummies. B) yeach!!!! C) a page in a book. D) I'd rather not describe the quiz, taking it is boring enough.

5) You are at question five and the quiz maker has run out of questions: A) Woo-hoo! B) Yes! Can I go now? C) 'C' is always the right answer, so I will answer 'C.' D) Perfect. I have run out of answers.

SCORING:

Give yourself one point for each time you answered. Then give yourself another point for each time you answered. Then give yourself as many points as you want! Congrats! You are now a wizard!!!!

IN YO' FACE!

26

Proper Clothing for
PARANORMAL
Investigations

You've prepared. You've done your research. It's time to suit up! Part of fighting the forces of the unknown means knowing what to wear at all times. When you're in the middle of a hot pursuit, you don't want an untied shoelace to trip you up! Here's a handy checklist of what you should wear:

1) <u>Form-Fitting Clothes</u>—Loose clothes always snag on branches, rocks, or nails when you're desperately trying to (tactically) run away.

2) <u>Quality Footwear</u>—For running, climbing, kicking. Also, get something with a distinctive tread, so you don't mistakenly start "tracking" yourself.

3) <u>Belt</u>—Good for holding items and tools you may need. Plus it's great for holding up your pants.

4) <u>Blue Pine Tree Hat</u>— The most important clothing item you can bring! Because, well . . . it's just really cool.

Mabel's Survival KNITTING!

How to survive in the wild with nothing but yarn!

We've all been there before: trapped in the wilderness, completely alone and without any sense of direction, and with only a ball of yarn as a companion. Here are some tips for surviving until the rescue dog arrives with his neck-barrel full of gummy bears:

Pass the Time! Knitting will not only help pass the time until someone comes to rescue you, but the repetitive knitting motions will help keep you calm and give you cool callouses.

Warmth! Okay, since no one has come to rescue you yet, you'll need to be prepared to stay the night outside. The best part about knitting is that you can make anything—hats, mittens, tents, sleeping bags, a boyfriend. Hey, why haven't I tried that yet?

Trail! Time to take matters into your own newly-knitted mittens! Try getting yourself un-lost by laying the yarn along the ground to make a trail. That way, you can always go back to where you were first lost, and make sure you're not walking around in circles.

Funny Wigs! When wandering around on your own doesn't work, and you realize you're more lost now than you were before, and you're probably going to starve or be eaten by a hawk or something, you're going to get a little kooky. Drape a bunch of loose yarn over your head like a wig and see if that fixes anything. Also, start talking to rocks.

Food! Boy, you're hungry. I mean, REALLY hungry. I guess you could eat yarn, right? Just a taste . . . just a . . .

lasso! Okay, okay, don't eat the yarn, it tastes horrible. Instead, make a loop in the yarn and lasso a wild animal, like a squirrel. Then eat it to survive!

leash! Who am I kidding . . . of course you can't eat a cute, lovable, adorable little woodland creature! Instead, make a leash with the yarn and have your new squirrel buddy lead the way to freedom!

I'M FUZZY!

You made it! Thank your cute new lifesaver by sharing a snack of mixed nuts. Then go take a shower. You've been trapped in the woods for days and you probably stink.

Dress Up Waddles!

Never leave a pig behind! Waddles wants to investigate your paranormal findings, too. Plus, he'll add an adorable factor of A BIllION!

Draw stylish clothes for Waddles to wear, like a hat, sweater, sunglasses, or boots:

Mabel's PUMP UP THE FUN Challenge, Clothing Edition

⠰⡵⡶⬦⬰

Time to set some more records! Try the challenges below and record your results:

How many socks can you fit over one foot?_____
(Your feet . . . will be . . . INVINCIBLE!)

How many hats can you stack on your head?_____
(Each one makes you cooler!)

How many sweaters can you put on and wear all at once?
_____ ⠰⡶⡵⬦⡵⠰⬤⡙

How long can you keep them on?_____
(For an extra level of
difficulty, attempt
outside in the summer.)

⡙⬤⠸ ⡙⬢⡞

⬠⬤
⬰⬤⡵⡵⠤

31

SUIT UP! Getting Your Gear Together

Got the clothes? Now you'll need the equipment:

1) <u>Flashlight</u>—Darkness is a monster's best friend.

2) <u>Camera</u>—Who's going to believe you without proof?

3) <u>Mirror</u>—To see that monster creeping behind you.

4) <u>Walkie-Talkie</u>—Communication is important.

5) <u>"Disco Girl" BABBA CD</u>—. . . What's this doing in here? That . . . uh . . . must be Mabel's, haha. Let's change the subject.

6) <u>Mysterious Journal You Found in the Woods</u>— What, you don't have one?

Grappling Hook!

The most useful thing in the whole entire world is obviously a grappling hook. I know what all the parts are called, but Dipper thinks his terms are more "educationally appropriate."

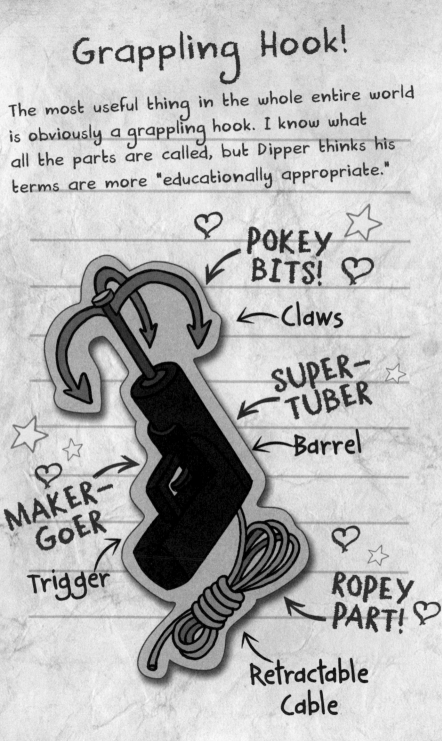

POKEY BITS!

← Claws

SUPER-TUBER

← Barrel

MAKER-GOER

Trigger

ROPEY PART!

Retractable Cable

Your Base of Operations

(a.k.a. Home Base, HQ, the Hideout, the Lair)

Whatever you choose to call it, you'll need a place to plan your missions and to retreat to when you're in trouble. (Mabel and I chose to call ours Pinesbase Delta 12.)

Where to Build It:

1) DON'T build it where your enemies would expect it. They'll expect to find it there.

2) DON'T build it where your enemies would least expect it. Your enemies are clever. They'll expect to find it where they'd least expect to find it.

3) DO build it somewhere in the middle of the enemy expectation range.

4) DO build it somewhere you can hear your mom, dad, or great uncle call you in for dinner.

5) DON'T build it somewhere your great uncle can find it and make you clean up the Mystery Shack gift shop.

Bad Choice for Lair

What to Build It With:

1) Use the world around you. A hollow tree trunk can be a good start for an awesome hideout. Or a cave that isn't occupied by a bear (or Multi-Bear). If your dog spends most of his time inside, why not convert his doghouse?

2) Choose something solid. Wood is good. A titanium alloy is better. If it's an emergency, you can use the cardboard box that the new fridge came in, but upgrade as soon as possible.

3) Use the seasons. Autumn leaves can be raked up to conceal the entrance of your hideout. A snow fort is a great option for winter operations. If you're desperate, you can lie in a puddle with a snorkel during a rainstorm.

My Ultimate Hideout

—The walls would be invisible from the outside and covered with maps of the world on the inside. It would have a telescope, seismograph, Geiger counter, and a Tiger Fist arcade game.

Use the rest of this page to draw what your secret hideout would look like. Don't forget to stock it with your favorite equipment.

Mabel's Guide to Successful Sleepovers

What good is having a great headquarters like Pinesbase Delta 12 (a.k.a. our bedroom in the Mystery Shack) if you can't share it with your friends? And what better way to share it than to have a sleepover!

HIP HOP

Essential Supplies

Pillows, sleeping bags, pet pig, various snacks, fake tattoos, hairbrush and curlers, makeup for makeovers, makeup for monster costume to scare brother, toothpaste, Candy, and Grenda (you may substitute your own friends if necessary).

Top Five Topics for Discussion

1) Boys—Cute or the CUTEST?!
2) Marshmallows—How many can we fit in our mouths?
3) Truth or Dare or Don't! (Candy always chooses "Don't.")
4) Wearing each other's clothes. We. Are so. CRAZY!!
5) Morphing into animals. If we try hard enough, I bet we can do it.

❤ BEST FRIENDS! ❤

Schedule of Sleepover Events:

09:00 PM Welcome guests

09:15 PM Sing pop songs till Dipper flees the bedroom

09:45 PM A light snack

10:15 PM Another light snack

10:30 PM Stop kidding yourself and eat the rest of the snacks

11:00 PM Tell Grunkle Stan that you are going to sleep

11:15 PM Sneak downstairs to spy on Grunkle Stan

11:20 PM Run back upstairs when caught

11:30 PM Settle into sleeping bags

11:35 PM Have deep discussions (see topics on previous page)

12:05 AM Fall asleep for the first time

12:15 AM Deny that you fell asleep

12:45 AM Fall asleep for the second time

01:00 AM Have spontaneous dance party to keep awake

01:12 AM Sneak downstairs to spy on Grunkle Stan

01:30 AM Fall asleep for the third time on the living room carpet, waiting for Stan

09:15 AM Get woken up as Stan trips over your sleeping body

MABEL'S SEAL of QUALITY

YOU'RE A STAR

GRAVITY FALLS and Other Places to Be Paranoid

When you're an experienced Paranormal Expert (Or P.E., as we like to refer to ourselves. Actually, that reminds me of gym class. Forget it!), you know that you can encounter the supernatural anywhere. Nevertheless, there are certain places that seem to be hotbeds of mystical activity.

Gravity Falls ranks among the weirdest places in the world. Let's begin with the start of the town itself. It was founded by the secret eighth-and-a-half president of the United States, Quentin Trembley, after he was driven from office in disgrace for trying to eat the White House. Trembley literally fell into the valley where Gravity Falls is now located and wrote the town charter while suffering from the resulting concussion. Other highlights from town history include giving beavers the right to vote in 1922 and being the first and only city to outlaw "Moon People." (So far, it's worked!) I had a brief chance to speak with Mr. Trembley after he escaped from a block of peanut brittle and we had the following chat:

Lessons Learned from the Eighth-and-a-Half President

An Interview with Quentin Trembley

D: Why do you hate pants?

Q: Pants are about restrictions. America is about freedom! This is why I issued the Depantsipation Proclamation! Down with pants!

D: What's your favorite food?

Q: Waffles! But don't get me started on pancakes . . . I waged war against them!

D: Do you always ride horses backwards?

Q: Of course! How else would you be able to see where you've been?

D: What lessons have you learned from being president?

Q: Never arm wrestle with a hammerhead shark! But do make them your Secretary of Defense!

D: Do you have a favorite color?

Q: Sure do!

D: Umm . . . okay. What is it?

Q: Triangles!

D: So, as a recap, we have learned absolutely nothing from the eighth-and-a-half president.

Q: TREMBLEY, AWAY!

NO PANTS

PRESIDENT MABEL's Top Five New laws to Make Everything Great!

As I'm sure you all know, President Trembley made me into an actual congressman. Congresswoman? Congressgirl? I headed straight to D.C. with a bunch of sharpened #2 pencils, three new notebooks, a special sweater for my first day, and a kazoo for debates. But those dopes in Congress wouldn't give me a desk! Not even a tiny one like poor Rhode Island.

I figured the only way to get things done in Washington is to get elected president. Here is my platform:

1) Everyone gets a barbecue apron with President Mabel's picture

2) Tax refunds will be delivered in the form of hot fudge sundaes

3) Pigs are now able to be vice president, secretary of state, or hogmaster general

4) Uncles who yell at their nieces will have to drive a clown car full of at least 100 clowns

5) Statewide pie-eating contests will be held to elect each governor

6) All teenage boys must address the president as "Sweetheart in Chief"

7) Top five lists now come with seven items listed

LAKE GRAVITY FALLS is not for the faint of heart. There are treacherous waterfalls, hidden caverns, and a hovering island-face that once tried to eat my boat. All kinds of supernatural sea creatures inhabit these waters, including the legendary Gobblewonker! On the plus side, the fishing is really good.

Can you help Soos pilot our boat safely through the many perils of Lake Gravity Falls?

Diagram of the Bottomless Pit
By Soos

Top of the pit. My advice: stay at
the top and don't fall in.

Middle of the pit.
Somewhere between two
and infinity miles deep.

Bottom of the pit. When you get to the
bottom, you get spit back out at the top.
There's some weird fourth-dimensional
stuff going on in this pit, dude.

WEIRD Places Around the World

BERMUDA TRIANGLE

An area of the Atlantic Ocean near Florida where numerous ships and planes have mysteriously disappeared. The pilots and crews of those craft have never been found. I wonder if my left sock that went missing last laundry day ended up in the Bermuda Triangle. Maybe that's where ALL missing socks go!

AREA 51

A secret military base in Nevada, Area 51 is rumored to have evidence of UFOs. Some believe the US government is testing top-secret alien technology to experiment to create spaceships, weather controlling equipment, and even teleportation machines. Of course, the government denies all knowledge of such things, which means they totally exist, right?!

EASTER ISLAND

Strange statues of human figures with large heads seem to grow out of the ground around the coast of Easter Island. These statues are hundreds of years old and can weigh up to eighty tons. Creating and moving such enormous statues back before machinery and powered tools were invented was an incredible task. Unless they're not actually statues, and instead, they're giant rock people growing right out of the ground! I think I'm on to something here. . . .

ATLANTIS

Legend tells that the island city of Atlantis suddenly sunk into the ocean. The whole island! Some believe that the people on the island learned how to live underwater and that Atlantis is now a thriving underwater city somewhere at the bottom of the ocean. Maybe that's where the people who've gone missing in the Bermuda Triangle end up!

STONEHENGE

A circle of mysterious stone pillars that is thousands of years old. No one knows why prehistoric people built such a place. The reason it is there and what it was used for is a complete mystery. I bet it has something to do with the giant rock people growing out of the ground at Easter Island. Or a communication beacon for

the underwater people of Atlantis! Or proof of an alien visit, like a crop circle, only made out of stone! There are so many possibilities!!!

MONSTERS and GHOSTS

The supernatural world is full of beasts of all shapes and sizes. I won't say that I've encountered and defeated them all, but I've taken down my fair share. If you run into these tough customers, this quick rundown may save your neck.

Dipper's Creaturepedia

Gnomes

Habitat: The forest (the sparkly section)

Known for: Being masters of disguise and vomiting rainbows

Fun fact: Much like ants, they can lift twenty times their own weight

Weakness: Leaf blowers

The Multi-Bear

Habitat: The darkest cave on top of the tallest mountain

Known for: Having six, no wait, seven . . . maybe eight heads?

Fun Fact: Head four is the least liked by the other heads

Weakness: Is a sucker for the music of Icelandic pop sensation BABBA

The Gremloblin

Habitat: Prefers bogs and marshes

Known for: Smelling boggy and marshlike

Fun Fact: Look into his eyes and see your worst nightmare!

Weakness: Easily distracted by motorized talking fish

The Weird, Naked Candy-Stealing Creature

<u>Habitat</u>: Bedroom closets and kitchen cupboards

<u>Known For</u>: Eating all of your Summerween candy

<u>Fun Fact</u>: You can kick him and he'll bounce like a dodgeball

<u>Weakness</u>: Tooth decay

Ma and Pa

<u>Habitat</u>: The abandoned Dusk 2 Dawn convenience store

<u>Known for</u>: Being ghosts, hating teenagers

<u>Fun Fact</u>: They love little children

<u>Weakness</u>: Unknown

What?!? "Weakness unknown"???!! My brother is being falsely modest here!

47

WEAKNESS REVEALED!!!

The totally true story of how my brother, Dipper, defeated the Dusk 2 Dawn ghosts.

Ma and Pa Duskerton were total suckers for cutesy little kid stuff. I could've won 'em over easily but I was off on a fantastical adventure with my pal Aoshima.

So Dipper stepped in and knocked their ghostly socks off with . . .

The LAMBY LAMBY DANCE!

Now let's all take a second to really get in a good laugh. I'll start us off . . . BWAHAHAHAHAHAHAHAHAHAHAHAHA!!!

Getting the Best of the BEAST

Being familiar with the different kinds of monsters is important, but knowing how to handle them is essential. Think you're ready? See if you can guess the CORRECT answer to each!

1) **The worst bite is:** A) from a werewolf. B) from a vampire. C) from a zombie. D) from your sister.

2) **Bigfoot is on one side of the forest clearing. The Abominable Snowman is on the other. You are in the middle. You:** A) start snapping photos. B) look for a bush to hide in. C) introduce them to each other. D) start a fight between them.

3) **A witch offers you your choice of three enchanted objects. You pick:** A) the Golden Toaster. B) the Never-Ending Yo-Yo. C) the Gossiping Elk's Head. D) all of the above. E) none of the above.

4) **The best time to confront a vampire is:** A) during daylight hours. B) at the stroke of midnight. C) before your bedtime. D) after you've taken a garlic-scented bath.

More quiz on the next page.

5) You are in the Gremloblin's cave, but he has fallen asleep. You should: A) tiptoe past him to the exit. B) wake him up to say good-bye. C) listen to him sleep-talking. Guy has some serious issues! D) snuggle up beside him and catch a few Z's yourself.

6) The ghoul that has you in his clutches won't stop talking about his evil plan. You: A) tell him to shut up and eat you already. B) point out the flaws in his plan and brainstorm with him about possible fixes. C) offer him a breath mint. D) keep him talking as long as possible.

Soos: Handyman of Mystery—How to Track Otherworldly Creatures

Yo! Dipper and I are, like, primo monster hunters. We captured the Gobblewonker, although that turned out to be fake. . . . Oh, and we tracked down a real live puh-terodactyl! But then we had to run away from a real live puh-terodactyl. . . . Well, as you can see, monster tracking is tricky. Keep the following tips in mind when you are trying to get all up in some creature's biz:

DO shower beforehand. Most creatures got powerful noses and you don't want your stank ruining your element of surprise!

DON'T freestyle rap. Even though I'm really really good at rhyming, monsters are not yet ready for my fresh jams. (Although they do like jars of fresh jams.)

DON'T call the monster "Dawg." Unless the monster is Cerberus, the multiheaded dog monster of ancient lore. Then "Dawg" is very appropriate!

DO wear a giant green T-shirt with a question mark on it. It makes you look mysterious—which chicks love—and alerts the monster to the fact that you mean business. Also, it's great camouflage if you're in the Mystery Shack.

DO bring some way to trap the creature. I recommend using a trap. Yelling "Gotcha!" or "You're coming with me!" is not as effective as you might think.

What to Say When You Encounter a MONSTER

You've finally found the thing. It's big, it's hairy, it's drooling, and it's waiting to make your acquaintance! When you first encounter a new monster, you may be at a loss for words. Being scared, amazed, or just plain confused can make you blurt out some weird stuff. Here are some lines I've heard when seeing a real monster for the first time:

Please don't eat me whole. Or . . . at all, I suppose.

AAAAAHHHH!!! It's so CUTE! I just want to rub balloons on its fur and watch them stick!

53

Turn That Beast . . .
into a BFF!

Here are some tips for turning a scary encounter with a monster into a friend-portunity:

1) DO stand up straight, offer your hand, and introduce yourself.

2) DON'T run away screaming. The monster's natural instinct to chase you will kick in, like a dog with a car.

3) DO laugh at their jokes.

4) DON'T laugh at their origin story. The tragic tale of how they became the unholy wretch you see before you is not meant as a gag.

5) DO invite them over to your house.

6) DO let your parents know they are coming over.

7) DON'T insist they come over if any torch-carrying mobs have gathered on your front lawn.

Mabel's "Insta-Pet"

So what do you do if, hypothetically, you aren't able to make friends with that monster and, hypothetically, all your normal friends are out of town and, hypothetically, your pet pig is mad at you because you've spent the last eight hours dressing him up and rehearsing for his one-act play "Abra-HAM Oink-coln"?

Don't fret! Use one of the following as an Insta-Pet (patent also pending):

1) Pet Pencil!

This is really two pets in one if you think of the two ends as two distinct personalities. There's Sharps Mclead, the no-nonsense hardhead who always gets to the point. And then there's Pinkie, his lovable, softheaded sidekick.

2) Pet Cap!

Not to be confused with the "Pet Cap" from Mabel's "Insta-Hat" (patent still pending). Got a hat? Take it off your head and cuddle it as if it were your pet!

3) Pet Crumply!

Take this page, tear it out, and crumple it up. Don't say I never gave you anything, 'cause I just gave you an amazing pet.

♥ PINKIE

SHARPS!

This side of the paper is Crumply's butt.

But seriously, tear this page out for a quick, fun new crumpled-up piece of paper/pet!

MANOTAUR MAZE

Manotaurs are a lot like Minotaurs but with even more body hair. There's less emphasis on mazes and more emphasis on nachos. If you want to hang out with them, then you will have to complete a huge number of "tasks" with a lot of senseless pain. Trust me, twelve hours of foosball? NOT worth it.

Only one path can lead you out of the Manotaur's labyrinth. Can you figure out which one to follow? (Note: If you can't, you're probably a Manotaur.)

Soos: Handyman of Mystery—How to Make an Upside-Down Box of Magic

Here's how to freak out your friends by turning the world upside down—and you won't even need superpowers!

What You'll Need:

A can with a plastic top and metal bottom. Think coffee can or one for oatmeal or potato chips.

A marker and a ruler. There's some precision work ahead, dude.

A roll of tinfoil. Sorry, but there might not be any extra left for hats this time.

Black construction paper.

Masking tape.

A sewing needle. A #10 sewing needle if you want to get extra precision points.

An adult. Again, there are pointy things being used.

What You Do:

Step 1—Empty out the can. I'm going with a potato chip can. Again, eating contents is not mandatory, but recommended.

Step 2—Draw a line around the can about two inches up from the bottom. (Told you that precision would play a role.)

Step 3—Cut the can in two along the line or let your designated adult do this. (While you take a potato chip break.)

Step 4—Poke a small hole in the center of the metal bottom with the needle. Take it slow, dawg. You want it nice and smooth.

Step 5—Take the plastic lid and tape it in between the two sections of the can. If it's clear plastic, you'll need to add some wax paper to make it more obscure.

Step 6—Wrap the tinfoil around the can twice and tape it down. This keeps the light out of the tube.

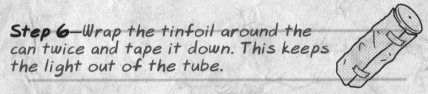

Step 7—Roll the construction paper into a tinier tube and insert it partway into the chip can. Now you got a light-shielding eyepiece. You are owning that light!

Step 8—Go outside on a sunny day and look through your eyepiece. What do you see?

Warning! Try not to freak out hard-core when you look into the box. The first time I did this I kept standing on my head to get the world to look right. The easier solution is to take your eye away from the eyepiece.

Dipper's Guide to Were-Anythings

Vampires, werewolves, girl scouts . . . there are many horrible creatures that try to bite you and make you join their unholy clan. But believe it or not, I have discovered several NEW classes of were-creatures, mentioned here for the first time!

1) **Were-Bear**—Just what it sounds like. Unless you like eating honey and walking around without wearing pants, don't get bitten!

2) **Were-Wife**—If she bites you, you're married for life. And the only possible divorce involves a wooden stake and a lot of emotional baggage!

3) **Were-Pig**—Found near haunted farms. Will make you sing "E-I-E-I-OHHH-NO!!"

~~4)~~ 3.5) Were-Pig?! Talk about a dream come true! I'm going to see if Waddles will bite me right now!

4) **Were-Man**—Actually, I think this is just a weird guy by the bus station who bites people. Nothing happens when he does it— but it hurts!

5) **Were-Waffle**—Never eat at Greasy's Diner. 'Nuff said.

Mabel update: I smeared peanut butter on me to get Waddles to bite me! Currently waiting to turn into a Were-Pig. Will update you on the situation!

GHOSTS

Introduction:

There are some in this world who are skeptical about the afterlife. I used to be one of those people (known in technical terms as "buzzkills") until I had a perspective-changing run-in with them. (Anything you've heard from Mabel about that incident is a filthy lie and should be forgotten immediately!) Since then, I've essentially become a ghost expert. . . .

Me too, dawg! I've watched about 8,000 hours of _Ghost Harassers_ and I've seen _Ghost Suckers_ and _Ghost Suckers II_ both in theaters. Can I be part of your ghost chapter, dude? Pretty please?

Uh . . . sure, Soos. Anyway, if you readers want to survive your encounter the way I did, you need to be prepared, be alert, beware . . . and believe!

Yeah! Also, be sure to read this section in a dark room with a lit flashlight pointing up to your face. I don't want to overpromise, but it will make this section, as we experts say, "Spooktacular."

Note: "Spooktacular" is not a scientific term.

ENSPOOKLOPEDIA BOO-TANICA

(Uh . . . Soos came up with the title.)

Here are a few terrifying examples of the poltergeistal horror lurking between the gossamer fabric of life and death!

1) <u>Shadow-Wraiths</u>: Reaper-like and cunning, these specters of the night linger among the shadows and love to play tricks on the eyes. Do you ever notice something move, but it's gone when you turn your head? You may have a Shadow-Wraith nearby.

2) <u>White-Sheet Willy</u>: The old standard. Apparently (I just learned this), many bedsheets have souls, and if you don't wash 'em enough, they turn into ghosts. Makes sense to me!

3) Banshees: Banshees are . . . you know what? I'm sorry, I just have to po out that the above claim is not substantiated by any kind of scientific resear Banshees are . . . some sort of evil lady-ghost. . . . I'm sorry, I lost my trai of thought here.

4) <u>Mr. Boo-Boo</u>: It's always a fun time when Mr. Boo-Boo is about! He's a "friendly" ghost who just wants to play, and his G-rated capers amuse the whole family! Don't forget hi catchphrase: "You trippin', Boo!"

5) <u>Poltergeists</u>: Okay, seriously, Soos. That's just from a movie.

6) <u>"School Spirit"</u>: That's a kind of ghost, right? Schools are a scary place, and when homecoming rolls around, rumor of a mysterious "School Spirit" are on everyone's mind! Go Gravity Falls High!

7) Okay, this list is over.

8) <u>"Ghost Writers"</u>: Sometimes, despite what it says on th cover, someone else writes sections of a book without cre These unsung heroes are called . . . hey Dipper, where are you going?

Unfinished Business

Okay, I've distracted Soos by turning on *Ghost Suckers III*. Now I can tell you about the important stuff. Ghosts are stuck on Earth, haunting the rest of us, because they have unfinished business or "baggage." Instead of attempting to fight or bust a ghost (which will usually get you trapped in some sort of afterlife situation), try helping them resolve their problems so they may pass to the afterlife and stop haunting your basement, rearranging your fridge magnets, or giving you wedgies.

<u>Here are some common ghost problems and how to solve them:</u>

1) Never found their reading glasses? Check on top of their head.

2) Missed the final episode of *Duck-tective*? Reenact the TV show with puppets.

3) Crashed their car into a tree? Cut down the tree as revenge.

4) Lost their actual baggage when flying to Gravity Falls? Have your sister design them fashionable ghost sweaters.

5) Could never say "Peter Piper Peeped a Pair of Paranormal Poltergeists" three times fast? Try it yourself and say the ghost is better at it than you are.

Tricksters, Cheats, and WORSE!

Ghosts are scary, but they don't usually seem to carry their brains with them to the afterlife. However, some paranormal creatures are smarter than you'd think. These creatures are clever and use lies, tricks, and secrets to fool you—which is why you'd better know about them!

Summerween Trickster

This mysterious force was created by gross discarded Summerween candy, and for reasons still unclear, it came to life to get revenge. Even though the Summerween Trickster says he wants to eat your candy (or even *you!*), what he really wants is a friend . . . to eat HIM. It's a pretty messed-up situation if you think about it. (Don't think about it!)

The Hide Behind

Notorious in the lumberjack world, the Hide Behind is a mysterious creature that creeps up on people in the woods from behind. It is able to hide behind anything—trees, rocks, bushes— making it very difficult to spot. Actually, it's never really been seen so it may not even exist!

Actually, don't look now, but there's something right behind you. . . .

Bill Cipher

Speaking of feeling watched, the strangest being I have ever encountered in my dreams or nightmares is a psychotic triangle with a snappy bow tie who calls himself "Bill Cipher." Bill is especially tricky to deal with because he knows how to get into your mind, which really puts you at a disadvantage when trying to outsmart him.

He seems to be a master of illusion and can make you believe things that aren't real. Remember, when dealing with someone as sneaky as Bill, quick and imaginative thinking is your best weapon against him.

Bill might make promises and offers that sound amazing. DON'T LISTEN TO HIM!! There is always some sort of tricky fine print that makes it a really bad deal. Plus, remember, IT'S ALL IN YOUR MIND! Bill doesn't exist in the physical world unless he tricks someone and gains control of their body. Believe me, you don't want Bill in your mind. He will wreck the place!

MABEl'S PUMP UP THE FUN CHALLENGE— Messing with People (or Monsters) Edition

Bleep Blop Bloop! Try to see how long people will let you get away with doing these annoying things:

How many hours can you go without saying anything at all before people start to worry you've turned into a mime?

How much bubble bath can you add to your bath before someone takes the bottle away? _____

How many high fives can you and a friend do in a row? My record is 45! _____

How many hugs can you give your brother before he bans you from his bedroom? _____

ORANGE YOU HAPPY MON?

What's Gotten INTO Me?

Possession: It happens, and it's ANNOYING. In the P.E. biz (okay, I've started using that term), you have to be on guard against foreign entities hoping to invade your personal space. (Like your body, for example.) If you're not feeling like yourself lately, use this quiz to tell whether you've been possessed by a ghost or a demon, or have just caught your sister's cold:

1) **When I sneeze:** A) snot comes out. B) ectoplasm comes out. C) fire comes out.

2) **My temperature is:** A) 99.2 degrees. B) 50 degrees. C) 3000 degrees hotter than the sun.

3) **My tongue:** A) is sore. B) has icicles hanging off it. C) is forked like a snake's.

4) **My head:** A) is stuffy. B) has its mouth open and is wailing uncontrollably. C) is spinning completely around in a circle.

5) **I have trouble sleeping because:**
   A) I keep tossing and turning.
   B) I keep floating up off the bed.
   C) the bed keeps floating up off the floor.

If you mostly answered **A:** take two aspirin and go to bed early. You'll be fine. If you mostly answered **B:** tell the ghost to vacate your premises and in return you'll help it with whatever's bothering it. (See Page 63.) If you mostly answered **C:** wait for your sister to bug you. The demon will then exit you and hopefully possess her instead!

Cleaning Up After a
SUPERNATURAL ENCOUNTER

1) <u>If you've driven away a yeti</u>—A common lint brush should take care of any leftover hair.

2) <u>If you've dispelled a ghost</u>—You'll want to use a bleach-free cleaner to get rid of the ectoplasm.

3) <u>If you have defeated a demon</u>—Make sure your fire extinguisher is fully charged. There will be a lot of localized fires to put out.

4) <u>If you've beaten a multidimensional monster</u>—There's no way to "clean up" the dimensional wormholes. Just put some caution tape around them till they close up on their own.

5) <u>If you've conquered the gnomes</u>—They have this sparkly discharge and that stuff gets everywhere. You're going to need a professional cleaning service.

Calming Down After a
SUPERNATURAL ENCOUNTER

Let's face it—sometimes it's hard to calm down after you've just battled the forces of evil. I know that I want to just go right into a debrief meeting at Pinesbase Delta 12. But whenever I say the word "debrief," Mabel just laughs at me. So I've learned that it's better to just try to relax. But to be honest, I'm pretty tense all the time. So I've asked Wendy to write a few pages about how to decompress after a supernatural adventure. ◇ꝏ▽

Wendy's Guide to Relaxing

Hey, guys. So Dipper asked me to write about relaxing, but what he calls "relaxing" is what I call "slacking." The first rule of slacking is not doing work. And writing something for someone else sounds a lot like work. So I'm taking the day off instead and accepting Stan's bribe to let him have the next few pages so he can write . . .

ꝏ

ꝏꝏꝏ

ꝏꝏꝏ

MR. MYSTERY'S PAGES OF INTRIGUE AND OPPORTUNITY

Sponsored by Gravity Falls' Number ≠ 1 attraction—the Mystery Shack!!

The Mystery Shack is an Exciting Adventure-torium™* where you will encounter several thousand bizarre AntiquCuriosities™ never before gazed upon by man, woman, or full-price-paying child.

Included in the Low-Low-Low Price of Admission are:

* 1. Mystery Entrance
* 2. Mystery Outhouse
* 3. Ambience
* 4. Free Oxygen
* 5. Whatever Lies Inside!!!???!?!?

MYSTERY COUPON

$1 $$$ $1

GOOD FOR ONE DOLLAR!*

*ADDED TO THE PRICE OF ADMISSION

$1 $1

(*Say that out loud and you owe me ten dollars!)

70

Come down to
THE MYSTERY SHACK

and behold it ALL with your very own eyes!

BEWARE!

The Mystery Shack is not for those who are faint of heart or light of wallet.

Answer the questions posed below before venturing into the dark, dank* dungeon of de-strangement that is the Mystery Shack!

To Explore the Unknown, I will pay:
A) exactly $15.99. B) as little as I can get away with. C) any price that is asked of me.

When I think of Mr. Mystery, I think of:
A) the handsome guy leading this tour. B) the charlatan who stole my wallet. C) the legendary explorer who has brought the wonders of the world together under one roof for all to enjoy.

A sign reads "No Photographs." I: A) put my camera away. B) turn off the flash and try to sneak a photo or two. C) tip my tour guide for making such an excellent sign!

I have wandered beyond the cautionary ropes erected for my protection and scratched my arm on the claw of the mighty Sascrotch. I shout out: A) "Does anyone have a bandage?" B) "You will be hearing from my lawyer!" C) "How lucky to have encountered such a magnificent beast and lived to tell the tale!"

If you mostly answered A, please proceed and FunJoy ™ yourself!
If you mostly answered B, I sense that you are not in tune with the Mysteries of the Universe. Please return when you are feeling more receptive.
If you mostly answered C, you are eligible for membership in Mystery Shack Gold, an exclusive club where you pay more and we are extremely grateful.
If you answered "none," you're an undercover cop! Got a warrant? Didn't think so, pal! Get off my property before you have an "accident" in the Bottomless Pit!

*We are working on the smell. A plumber has been called.

RUBBER MONSTER HANDS

Trick gullible nephews into thinking there's a monster on the loose.

Also good for loosening tight jar lids.

Item No. 607

$9.99

MYSTERY SPECS

What Mysteries of the Universe will be revealed? Why are you asking me?

Buy the glasses and find out for yourself.

Item No. 113

$7.25

OFFICIAL POLICE HANDCUFFS

From all states and localities.

Slightly used.

Item No. 911

$12.05

WORLD'S MOST DISTRACTING OBJECT

Hypnotize your friends, your neighbors, your . . .

What was I writing about again?

TEACUP MONKEYS

Real, live, NOT fake, actual pets that you grow in your own teacup

$6.99

Item No. 454

MYSTERY SHACK ASSUMES NO LIABILITY FOR ANY ACCIDENTALLY CONSUMED MONKEYS.

SURPRISE BAGS!!!

Each black nylon bag is filled with mysterious objects and smells.

For pickup only, oustide the back of the Mystery Shack.

$2.00

Item No. 733

SMOKE CLOUD

Annoying employees, cloying kids, disgruntled customers! Use Smoke Cloud to escape them all.

Item No. 200

MYSTERY [SOAP]

Use in bathroom to hilarious effect. Turns hands and face blue! Cheap!

Item No. 667

15¢

INDUSTRIAL STRENGTH SOAP

Permanent blue stains on hands or face? This soap and only this soap will get rid of them.

$15.00

Item No. 668

SOAP

IS YOUR MONEY HAUNTED?!???

Yes! Yes, most definitely it is. That's why you need STAN PINES'S MONEY PURIFiCATION SERVICE!

It's a little-known fact, but any denomination that features a picture of a dead president is actually haunted! And you don't want ghost money. Trust me.

So send it in to me, Stan Pines, to be cleansed, purified, and rid of ghosts forever! And it's practically FREE*! This is totally a real thing and NOT a scam! Seriously!

*Money purification process actually costs $10 per each $10 purified. No refunds or exchanges. Ghost-purification not guaranteed.

GRUNKLE STAN'S CHUCKLE BARREL FULL O' BELLY BUSTERS

Don't ever say your Grunkle Stan never gave you anything for free. Don't like these jokes? Tough! You get what you pay for, Mr. Critical.

WHAT DO YOU CALL A PAIR OF FREE IN-LINE SKATES?

CHEAPSKATES!

HOW MANY TOURISTS DOES IT TAKE TO SCREW IN A LIGHTBULB?

IF I TELL 'EM THE LIGHTBULB IS ACTUALLY A MINI SUN AND CHARGE 'EM TWENTY DOLLARS TO TOUCH IT, WHO CARES?!

WHAT DID THE LAWYER NAME HIS DAUGHTER?

SUE.

KNOCK., KNOCK..

Who's THERE?

LAZY EMPLOYEE.

LAZY EMPLOYEE WHO?

GET BACK.TO WORK!

WHY DID THE SKELETON GO ALONE TO THE DANCE?

BECAUSE HE HAD NO BODY TO GO WITH HIM.

WHAT DID THE JACKALOPE SAY TO THE SASCROTCH?

SEE YOU AT THE MYSTERY SHACK!
WHERE WONDER AND BEFUDDLEMENT BECOME
BE-WONDERFUDDLLE-MENT™!!!!!!

Ha-ha!
You're a RIOT!!

–Soos

(Mr. Pines paid me five
bucks and a candy bar
to say that.)

Okay, before we move on, let me first apologize for what just happened on the preceding pages. When Mabel and I decided to do this guide, we both agreed that Grunkle Stan would not get anywhere near it. I would edit his stuff out, but Stan threatened to "pull publication" of the book, which I think means that he would grab it and lock it in his safe.

He also insisted that I include this "completely accurate" drawing of him.

It just goes to show that a P.E. should always expect the unexpected. In the next chapter, we discuss the wider world of stranger supernatural dangers that exist alongside your garden-variety ghosts and ghouls.

The Unnatural Supernatural

Underwater Encounters

Large bodies of water can be scary places. Who knows exactly what hides beneath the wavy surfaces of lakes, ponds, seas, oceans, or even moderate-sized puddles?

The Gobblewonker

A legendary sea monster that was rumored to live in Lake Gravity Falls. Even though we disproved the existence of this monster by discovering it was actually a giant robot piloted by Old Man McGucket, some claim that the real beast is still swimming undiscovered at the bottom of the lake.

Octopossum

An eight-headed aquatic possum creature that scares sunbathers and is really good at playing dead. Some say that this beast mutated thanks to the toxic runoff from the Northwest Industries Mudflap Company. Still others say it's just eight regular possums stuck to a very large wad of gum.

Bloody Murray

Rumor has it that the ghost of an old bait and tackle shop owner named Murray haunts Lake Gravity Falls. If you're near the lake and say "Bloody Murray" three times while spinning around in a circle, he'll appear! However, he's kind of an annoying old man who really wants you to buy his worms, so conjuring him is not advised. Unless you really want some worms.

Merpeople

Merpeople are more human than fish. Except for their lower halves. That's, well, that's like 100 percent fish. They smell like a seafood restaurant and if you ever have the opportunity to perform reverse CPR on one, DON'T.

Hold the phone, Dipper! You know nothing about the wonderful and beautiful Merpeople!

Mabel! I'm in the middle of something! Sorry about that. Apparently Mabel thinks she can hijack this chapter! Well, Stan's intrusion was all I can stand! I will not let Ma

All right, Candy and Grenda are overpowering Dipper with a level-three tickle attack. He should be out of our hair while I tell you about Merpeople:

They're AWESOME! I met this one Merguy named Mermando and he was pretty much the best boy I've ever met! But I've met lots of boys in Gravity Falls. Some wonderful, like Mermando, and some . . . not so much. Let's gossip about them! Turn the page already!

GRAVITY FALLS
"Yeah or Bleah" list

MABEL'S
SEAL OF QUALITY

Ever wonder who are Gravity Falls' cutest cuties? And bleahest bleahies? Find out here:

◇⋂♭Ɡ⌐

The YEAHS!

Mermando—His tan skin . . . His long, beautiful hair . . . His almost mustache . . . If it weren't for his constant need to be in water, this would be the boy for me!

◇⋄△▽�⋂▽

Norman—You know how we all have an idea of who the perfect boy is, but he never lives up to what's in your mind? That's Norman.

Greggy C, Creggy G, Leggy P, Chubby Z, and **Deep Chris**—Although they're all simple-minded clones, I would totally date any of the band members from Sev'ral Timez. I sure hope they're doing okay living out in the wild. I heard one of them was seen eating the old gum from the underside of a picnic table.

▽�’⋂⋂

★ SEV'RAL TIMEZ

The Bleahs . . .

Gideon—His big white hair, shortness in stature and attitude, and his extreme hatred for my family are huge turnoffs. He does get points for his Waddles-like pig nose, though. So cute!

Gnomes—The multiple gnomes that made up "Norman" are just not as attractive as the mysterious, potential hottie vampire I thought "Norman" was. Bleah!

Robbie—I just don't get what some girls see in him. I mean, he's all tight jeans, angsty attitude, and guitar. Hmmm . . . actually, maybe I need to rethink my list . . .

Vampire Boyfriends— Is He to Un-DiE For?

What happens if you stumble upon every girl's dream—a VAMPIRE BOYFRIEND?! Here's a handy-dandy quiz to see whether you have attracted the right sort of undead boyfriend.

Your new spooky boo is going to be at least a few hundred years old—that's a given. But the important thing is, how old does he act and look?

1) **My vampire boyfriend:** A) has a beautiful, lustrous head of hair. B) has coal-black eyes and chalk-white skin. C) has giant bat ears and six-inch-long fingernails.

2) **He prefers to wear:** A) the latest trends. B) a tuxedo and cape. C) a weird overcoat buttoned all the way up to his neck.

3) **My vampire boyfriend drives:** A) an Italian sports car. B) some kind of weird cross between a coffin and a drag racer. C) nothing. He prefers to fly everywhere.

YUM

4) Our dates take place: A) during the day, but we keep to the shadows. B) when the moon is full and the creatures of the night are howling. C) exclusively in a swirling pit of death and horror.

5) When we argue: A) he gets all angsty like a teenager. B) he tries to hypnotize me into obeying his will. C) he locks himself in his coffin and won't come out.

6) When we discuss our relationship: A) he promises me he'll love me forever. B) he starts talking about his past girlfriends, going back all the way to the 1700s. C) he gets that "bitey" look in his eyes.

7) When I drag him into a sunny field of flowers for an afternoon picnic: A) he sparkles like an angel. B) he hisses and runs into the forest. C) he turns to dust. Whoops!

SCORING:

Give yourself one point for each time you answered A, two for B, three for C, and then total your score.

7–11 Points—Congrats, friend! This one is a keeper. A CRYPT-keeper! Just like the main character in my favorite book, *True Vampire Blood: The Diary Journal Chronicles: Sequel Moon Descending!*

12–16 Points—Sounds more like an eccentric uncle than a boyfriend. Don't date him. Have him perform magic tricks at your birthday party instead.

17–21 Points—Yikes! leave this creep in the crypt where you found him. Or poke him with a stick.

Monster Fashion Show!

Hi. Mabel's best friend Candy, here.

AND GRENDA! Mabel's other best friend! WE'RE FASHIONISTAS HERE TO JUDGE THE GRAVITY FALLS MONSTERS ON THEIR FASHION SENSE.

The monster with the best outfit wins our coveted Most Monsterlicious Monster award.

Here we go!

FIRST UP IS THE SIX-THOUSAND-YEAR-OLD MUMMY! SHE'S LOOKING AS THIN AS EVER—PRACTICALLY ALL BONE. GROSS. Next please!

Her rags have a nice, loose fit, but they are sooo six thousand years ago.

NEXT UP IS THE WEREWOLF. IT LOOKS AS IF ALL HIS CLOTHES WERE TORN OFF DURING HIS TRANSFORMATION.

Hmmm, yes. Without proper attire, or any clothes at all, it seems we must disqualify the werewolf.

HERE COMES THE REANIMATED CORPSE OF A ZOMBIE. SUCH CONFIDENCE IN HIS WALK. SLOW. DELIBERATE. DID HIS LEG JUST FALL OFF?

The tattered remains of his rotten clothes are what I would call "fierce."

OH, YEAH. SO FIERCE.

I think we have our win—wait. Wait just a second. It looks like we have one final contestant.

PACIFICA NORTHWEST?!? THIS IS A FASHION SHOW FOR MONSTERS!

Then she fits right in! Pacifica Northwest wins the award for Most Monsterlicious Monster!!

Ewwww!!! Yuck! Blargh!!!!

I just got this creepy letter from the Gravity Falls Maximum Security Prison from you-know-who. I don't even want to write his name again and not in a he's-so-powerful-I-dare-not-invoke-it way. Just in a what-a-little-weirdo way. I'm going to put it inside here and never look at it again. I suggest you do the same.

GRAVITY FALLS
MAXIMUM SECURITY PRISON

US Penitentiary
PO Box 10•1•9•12
Gravity Falls, OR 26•9•16

ello, dearest Mabel,

ven though I am away, I wrote this short note to let you know I'm thinking of your
ovely face, and how I can get my revenge against you and the whole accursed
ines family. The warden keeps us all on a pretty tight schedule, but I try to find a little
Me time each day to reflect on what I've done wrong and how I can avoid rep-
Eating the same mistakes when I get out on parole and put my next
Evil scheme into action. Here's what a typical day looks like for me:

Sunrise and wake at 7 a.m. One-handed push-ups till 7:15. Bribe the guard for hair gel and
Comb at 7:20. Style hair from 7:25–8. Breakfast 8–8:30. (It's difficult staying on
A low-carb diet in here, but I must preserve my figure!) Rehabilitative Art
Program 9–11:30. Right now, I'm going through an abstract
Expressionist phase. Lunch is from 12–12:30. I eat a small salad and an
Orange. Twice a week I smash my potatoes into the face of the biggest guy at my table to
Reestablish my dominance. Free Play in the yard 12:30–1:30, where I like to sun-
Bathe and work on my gorgeous tan. Rehabilitative License Plate Making 2–5:30.
Evening meal from 6–7. (The chocolate pudding is my one weakness.) Bribe
Daniel, the guard, for latest issue of *Preacher's Digest* at 7:10. From 7:15–8 I read and
Even relax a bit before I plot my revenge from 8–9. Lights out at 9. Then I
Stew in hatred for most of the night and dream my funny little nightmares.
Though I cannot imagine how painful it will be to see your entire family destroyed
Right before your very eyes, I just want you to know that I will be there for you. Well,
Obviously I will be there, since I will be the one doing the destroying. I'm sure
You understand. But once we have the unpleasant business of your family's
Elimination behind us, I hope that maybe you'll consider giving me another chance.
Dinner and a movie, perhaps?

Yours Forever,

Lil' Gideon

Lil' Gideon

Inanimate Objects That May Be Planning Your Demise

Okay, I'm back. Candy and Grenda had me paralyzed with . . . uh . . . some sort of . . . dark magic. But I eventually outwitted them and got away. Or they got hungry and left. MOVING ON!

Inanimate Objects: things that can't think or move.

So what do you do when they *do* start thinking and moving?! One of the scariest things that can happen is when something you thought was not alive BECOMES alive! There are inanimate objects all around you that could suddenly come alive and attack—the chair you're sitting in, that snack you're eating, even this book! (Don't insult this book.)

But those are all pretty unlikely as far as inanimate objects go. The kinds of non-alive things that you should be suspicious of are as follows:

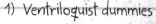

1) Ventriloquist dummies

2) Wax figures

3) That weird furnace that kind of looks like a face

4) Your favorite indoor plant

5) Dolls and action figures

6) Furniture with big cushions

7) Old paintings of creepy pec[...]

8) Any and all skeletons

Mabel's Craft Corner—
SOCK PUPPETS!

You know what's better than inanimate objects?
CUTE inanimate objects! like sock puppets!

Make your own sock puppet with
the following items!

1) Sock (preferably a clean one)
2) Colored markers (for decorating)
3) Yarn (for hair)
4) Googly eyes, if you have them.
   (If not, use buttons or draw
   on eyes with those markers!)
5) Hot glue gun (But you should
   probably use it with a grown-up.)

After you've created your own
cute sock friend comes the
important stuff: the personality!

1) Give your sock puppet friend a cute
   name! like Señor fuzzy Pants!
2) Find the right voice. Try doing a
   squeaky voice or a deep low one.
   Those are pretty much the options.
3) What are your sock puppet's
   favorite things to do? Dance? Herd
   sheep? Collect strange paintings
   of battleships?

SOCK PUPPETS

Well, for some reason Mabel has made a ton of sock puppets, and they're creeping me out. I feel like they watch me when I sleep and—did that one just blink? If they come to life, I'm officially moving out of this attic! Here are some tips on how to defeat evil, attacking sentient sock puppets:

1) Trick them into jumping into the washing machine. A good spin cycle will wash evil intentions away.

2) Find a loose thread and pull. The sock should unravel into a pile of string.

3) Blind them by popping off their googly eyes. However, they have a fantastic sense of smell, so they can still find you.

4) Wear them. They'll fight you the whole time, but if you can stick your foot inside them, you'll eventually stomp them out.

5) Tear them apart. I mean, they're just socks, I guess.

No sock puppet was harmed in the staging of this picture.

Is That Goat Watching Me?

Our goat, Gompers, is following me. At least, I think he's following me. Sometimes goats just look bored and chew on mouthfuls of grass, but what are they really thinking about? Are they thinking about you? Are they . . . watching you?

Answer the following True or False questions to know whether you are being spied on or just being paranoid:

1) The goat's gaze follows me as I walk across the yard. **T/F**

2) Most of my possessions are chewed up and have gray hair on them. **T/F**

3) I found hoofprints in my bedroom. **T/F**

4) When I look into the goat's eyes, I can see the future. **T/F**

5) When I go to sleep, I feel like a goat is watching me from the darkness of my closet. **T/F**

6) If I look over my shoulder really quickly, I am positive I saw the goat hide behind a tree to avoid being seen. **T/F**

7) When other people talk to you, all you hear is a goatlike "behhhh!" **T/F**

8) Whenever I discover a mystery, the goat always somewhere nearby, staring. **T/F**

9) Someone (or something) ate my secret stash of Summerween candy. **T/F**

10) I can't stop thinking about goats! **T/F**

(He's watching you . . .)

Answers: If you answered "TRUE" for most of the even-numbered questions, you're most likely being watched and followed by some sort of supernatural goat If you answered "TRUE" for most of the odd-numbered questions, you're probably just hanging around a normal goat and your sister is pranking you.

*Either way, I wouldn't trust that goat.

VIDEO GAMES—Real Danger from a Simulated World

Parents are always telling their kids to put down the video games and go outside. They think video games can be dangerous. And they're RIGHT!

If you accidentally bring a video game character to life (It happens!), here are some things you need to watch out for:

1) Pixel scrapes (They're sharp!)

2) Any boxes, barrels, or crates should be broken open to see what kind of power-ups are inside.

3) That same catchy music will loop over and over and you WILL get sick of it eventually.

4) Bad guy minions are easily defeated, but when you continue walking, more will always re-spawn.

5) Sixty-Four-Hit Epic Combo Knockouts. No one wants to get punched/kicked/head-butted sixty-four different ways.

6) One-dimensional characters. Meaning, the characters in video games are not very deep or interesting people to talk to. They only have one driving force, like avenging their dead father. And that's all they talk about! Physically, they're two-dimensional.

Lessons Learned from a
FIGHT FIGHTERS CHAMPION

An Interview with Rumble McSkirmish

D: What's your favorite food?
R: ANYTHING THAT CAN BE EATEN IS A POWER-UP!

D: Who would win in a fight, a grizzly bear or a shark?
R: HA HA HA. I LAUGH AT SUCH A FIGHT! I WOULD USE MY
SUPERIOR INTELLIGENCE AND STRENGTH TO BEAT UP BOTH THE
SHARK AND THE BEAR WITH A BASEBALL BAT, MAKING ME THE
ULTIMATE CHAMPION!!!

D: Okay, but if the fight was only between the shark and bear—
R: ULTIMATE CHAMPION!!!

D: What do you like to do for fun?
R: TRAVEL THE WORLD AND DEFEAT THE GREATEST FIGHT FIGHTERS!

D: What is your greatest accomplishment?

R: FINDING THE MAN WHO KILLED MY FATHER. WHICH I HAVE
NOT DONE YET. BUT WHEN I DO, IT WILL THEN BE MY GREATEST
ACCOMPLISHMENT! FATHER! I WILL AVENGE YOOOOU!!!

D: Right. Do you have any advice to give our readers?
R: WINNERS DON'T LOSE!

How to Make a Fashion Statement While Being INVISIBLE

MABEL'S SEAL of QUALITY

I think if I had to pick one magical ability, I would choose invisibility, hands down. When else can you parade around naked and not get yelled at?

ᕼᒷᕲᔕ

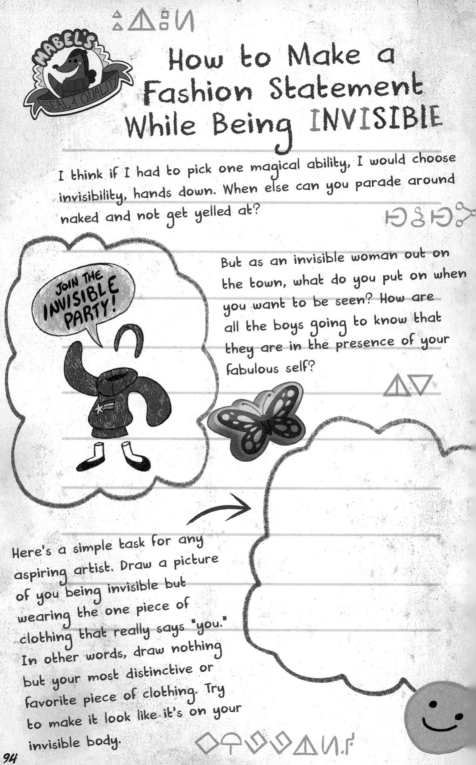

JOIN THE INVISIBLE PARTY!

But as an invisible woman out on the town, what do you put on when you want to be seen? How are all the boys going to know that they are in the presence of your fabulous self?

△▽

Here's a simple task for any aspiring artist. Draw a picture of you being invisible but wearing the one piece of clothing that really says "you." In other words, draw nothing but your most distinctive or favorite piece of clothing. Try to make it look like it's on your invisible body.

◇⊤◠♡◠△И⌐

Creature Communication

Monsters aren't easy to talk to, and not just because public education is really rare in haunted forests. Here are some hard-earned tips if you want to have a chat with your recently discovered monster:

1) **DO try English.** You'll be surprised how many monsters speak it.

2) **DO have a multilingual dictionary or a translator app on your phone.** If they don't speak English, your best bet is Spanish or (surprisingly) Esperanto.

3) **DON'T try to mimic their nonhuman language.** They'll think you are mocking them or you will mistakenly say something offensive.

4) **DO listen closely and record your conversation.** They may be speaking backwards.

5) **DO use hand gestures.** Also helpful with a monster who has sensitive hearing. If the monster has no face, tap a message in Morse code on his horrifying faceless head-mound.

6) **DON'T talk at all.** Just get out of there!

YOUR PET PIG—How to Interpret His Grunts, Groans, Snorts, and Snout Twitches

"Oink."
Translation:
"Hello, nice to see you."

"Oink?"
Translation:
"Would you like to scratch my belly?"

"Oink!"
Translation:
"Scratch my belly NOW!"

"Sniff, sniff, snort!"
<u>Translation:</u>
"I know there's a corn chip around here somewhere!"

"Snort, snurf, honk."
<u>Translation:</u>
"Cancel my three o'clock conference call."

"Weeh weeh weeh!"
<u>Translation:</u>
"You have frightened me. I shall stay here no longer."

Word Jumble

How many creepy words can you make using only the letters found in the following phrase?

PLEASE HELP! THIS IS NOT A WORD JUMBLE!

Answer: Hmm . . . I got "mold," "supermodel," "eel worms," "mouse pad," and "earlobes." But those aren't that creepy. I'm beginning to think this isn't a real word jumble.

What to Do When the MONSTER Is YOU

The last two chapters should have given you a good overview of how to confront, conquer, and control the various paranormal creatures that might cross your path. But what do you do if you or those you love are stricken with some sort of supernatural malady? For instance, if your friend Soos switches minds with a pig, do you try to switch him back or just accept the fact that he seems to be happier rolling in the mud than he ever was as handyman? This chapter will teach you how to deal with Body Switching, Shrink Rays, and other Body-Altering Phenomena. (We won't cover tattoos because there's no cure for being a poser. Ohhh! You just got zinged, Robbie!)

What to Do When You Wake Up as Your SISTER

I've seen some pretty horrifying stuff while living in Gravity Falls, but the scariest stuff I've encountered is when a supernatural change or transformation happens to *you*.

Without a doubt, the most terrifying change that has ever happened to me, by far, is when my sister and I *swapped bodies*. It was. The. Worst. Thing.

Here are a few tips on what to do if you are ever in a similar situation:

Tip #1—Don't panic! It's definitely the first thing you'll want to do, but you must keep a level head; otherwise, you might get sucked into a sleepover, makeover, or some other kind of terrible girl-related "-over."

Tip #2—Figure out what caused the switch. Did either of you discover a genie recently? Make a wish on a shooting star? Create a static charge on a body-swapping carpet? I would never purposefully wish to switch bodies with Mabel (and you shouldn't either!), but there's definitely some sort of magic or supernatural force happening, so the sooner you find the source, the sooner you're back to normal.

Tip #3—Stay in character. You'll essentially be "playing the part" of your sister, so you have to act like her to avoid suspicion. She'll have to do the same for you, otherwise, when you switch back, everyone will think the both of you have gone nuts. So remember to wear sweaters and say "boop" when you touch your nose. You know, girl stuff.

Tip #4—Okay, now you can panic. It's scary and frustrating being trapped in a girl's body! Especially your sister's! You're gonna need a little freak-out time.

Probably Dipper   Mabel?

Navigating the Room When You're Two Inches Tall

Potato Chip

Walking back from the kitchen to the chair in front of the TV doesn't sound too difficult, but imagine what that epic journey would be like if you were only two inches tall! Here's how to stay alive when you're the size of a potato chip:

1) **Don't get lost!** Everything will look drastically different from down there, so find the tallest point in the room as a reference point. A hanging lightbulb or that stain on the ceiling works great!

2) **Watch out for dust bunnies!** Balls of hair and dust can trap you and make your allergies go crazy.

3) **Watch out for pigs!** Pigs are notorious for eating most anything they can fit in their mouths. You're only potato chip sized. Don't be mistaken for tasting like one!

4) **Don't get stepped on!** But if you can't avoid it, try to get near that space by the heel of a dress shoe or in one of the treads of a sneaker.

5) **Carpets = jungles.** So don't get trapped in their gigantic fuzzy fibers!

6) **Catch a ride!** Hamsters, squirrels, and even large bugs make for great transportation. Like riding a horse, you'll get to your destination faster and probably have a blast while doing so!

THIS HAPPENED!

Ten Heads Are Better Than One—the Upside to Cloning Yourself

If you only get your information on cloning from TV or the movies, then you probably have a pretty negative view of the subject. But, speaking from personal experience, I will say that there isn't anyone out there that is going to "get you" like a clone will. Of course, the problems start when your clone actually wants to GET YOU so they can get rid of you and take over your life. Let's compare some of the good and bad things about cloning.

POSITIVE:

- Can do all your chores. Leaves you more time to focus on the important stuff.

- Likes the same games.

- Doesn't fight over what show to watch.

- Gets projects completed in half the time.

- Tries out a new haircut without messing up your own hair.

- Knows exactly what you're thinking. No more misunderstandings.

NEGATIVE:

- Won't do your chores. Just as stubborn and uncooperative as you are.

- All games end in a tie.

- Wants all your stuff.

- Looks at you weird.

- Will call the girl you like and ask her out before you have a chance to.

- Knows exactly what you're thinking! No way to outwit them!

When Dipper was dealing with his clone selves (I called them "Double Dippers" and he threw a shoe at me), at first it was hard to tell them apart. But any twin sister worth her sweaters can see the slight differences between those copies and "Dipper Classic." Can you help me pick out the real Dipper?

A.

B.

C.

D.

E.

F.

See PAGE 107 FOR THE ANSWER!

HOW MANY TIMEZ AM I GOING TO WRITE ABOUT CUTE BOY BAND CLONES? Sev'ral Timez!!!

Do you know what kinds of clones are boring? Dipper clones. Do you know what clones are AMAZING?!? Sev'ral Timez!!! It's a band made of cute clones!

Dipper says I'm "obsessive," but really, I just really, really, really like Sev'ral Timez! I read *Sev'ral Timez* magazine, have all their albums, and sing all their songs while staring at myself in the mirror! Here is a list of my favorite things about them:

<u>Favorite Song</u>: "Mabel Girl," 'cause they wrote it for me!

<u>Favorite Member</u>: It's so hard to choose! (Because they're literally all the same person.) But I gotta go with Deep Chris.

<u>Favorite Album</u>: CRAY CRAY

<u>Favorite Saying/lyric</u>: "We're nonthreatening!"

<u>Favorite Quirk</u>: They're all clones! How adorable!

GREGGY C

CREGGY G

CHUBBY Z

LEGGY P

DEEP CHRIS

What's your favorite band? How much do you know about them? Fill out the survey about your favorite band to see how much you know!

Favorite Band:_____

Favorite Song:_____

Favorite Member:_____

Favorite Album:_____

Favorite Saying/lyric:_____

Favorite Quirk:_____

Write a short paragraph about why you love this band so much! (Use the word "bodacious" for extra points!)

_____
_____
_____
_____
_____
_____

ANSWER TO PAGE 105: B

107

Dealing with
SHAPE-SHIFTERS

Definitely
NOT
Mabel

Unlike clones, who are actual copies of someone, shape-shifters are just jerks trying to fool you into thinking they're someone they're not. But just because your sister is acting extra weird, it doesn't mean she's been replaced by a doppelgänger*. Use the following flowchart to tell:

*If a shape-shifter of me were writing this, he would not use this kind of sophisticated foreign terminology.

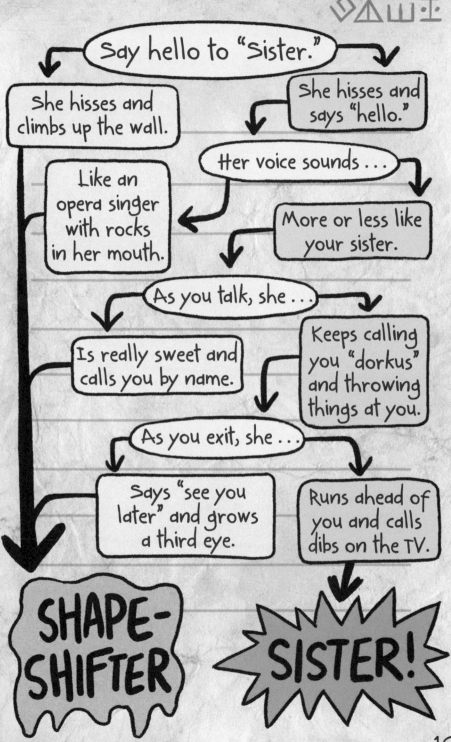

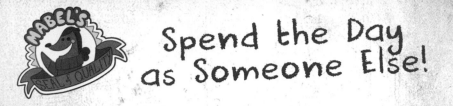

Spend the Day as Someone Else!

Pretend you are your brother (or sister or parent or pet). Dress up like them, imitate their voice, and do the things they like to do. Record your experiences and impressions below. What's it like to be someone else?

The Trouble with Time Travel

How to Avoid Paradoxes, Alternate Time Streams, and Your Past Self

Time travel seems like a great idea, right? If you could, why not travel past that big test you have on Friday and see what all the right answers are? Or leap back to the first day of school and start over? Or better yet, why not go back to the start of the summer and avoid school entirely for 3 months?

That sounds like a great idea, but what do you do when you run into *yourself* on opening day at the public pool?

Time travel comes with a lot of problems, paradoxes, and mind-numbing math. Puzzling through it all can give the novice traveler a horrible headache (referred to as a "timegraine"). Lucky for you, I've done my fair share of "Leaping." ("Voyaging"? "Trekking"? Write me if you have any suggestions for a cooler term than just "time traveling.") Anyway, I've learned the tricks of the time travel trade the hard way, and you are about to reap the rewards of all my experience. After reading this, you should have all you need to know to avoid the pitfalls and become a successful "Leaper." ("Voyager"? "Trekker"? "Journeyer"?)

Time Travel 101

The first part of successful time travel is knowing how to travel, of course. Well, the easiest way to travel is to get your hands on a time travel device (Figure 1). Doesn't sound easy, does it? Luckily for us, there are some pretty incompetent time travelers out there (Figure 2) and they always seem to be dropping their devices.

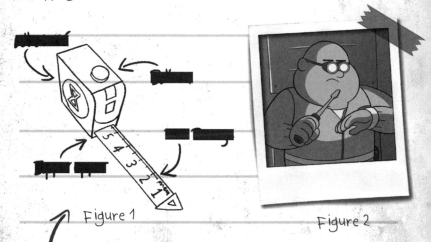

Figure 1

Figure 2

Let's examine this time travel device. Looks like a normal tape measure, right? But if you look more closely you'l

OKAY, OKAY. SORRY TO ALL THOSE READING THIS CHAPTER. HOW CAN I EXPLAIN THIS? OKAY—IT'S DIPPER WRITING THIS BUT NOT THE DIPPER WHO STARTED WRITING THIS CHAPTER. I'M DIPPER FROM THE FUTURE. I HAD TO LEAP BACK IN TIME (DECIDED TO GO WITH "LEAPING" AND "LEAPER.") AND STOP MY PAST SELF FROM GIVING YOU THE SECRETS OF TIME TRAVEL.

I COME FROM THE CALAMITOUS FUTURE WHERE TIME TRAVEL KNOWLEDGE IS COMMON. EVERYONE IS CONSTANTLY LEAPING BACK TO FIX EVERY LITTLE MISTAKE OR LEAPING FORWARD TO SEE WHAT HAPPENS ON THEIR FAVORITE TV SHOW. THE PARADOXES KEEP PILING UP AND THERE ARE SO MANY ALTERNATE TIME LINES! IT MAKES MY HEAD HURT JUST THINKING ABOUT IT.

SO I MUST STOP PAST DIPPER FROM COMPLETING THIS CHAPTER. IN FACT, IT WOULD BE SAFER IF I JUST BURNED THE ENTIRE BOOK. IF I AM SUCCESSFUL, THE HORRIFIC WORLD I LIVE IN WILL NEVER COME TO PASS. IN FACT, I SHOULD CEASE TO EXIST AS WELL. BUT I'M STILL HERE, SO DOES THAT MEAN I'VE ALREADY FAILED?? AGGH! MY HEAD IS THROBBING FROM ALL THIS TIME MATH!! I'M NOT SURE whe

Hi, everyone. You can ignore everything that Future Dipper was writing about. This is *Farther in the Future Dipper* and in my time all the troubles of Future Dipper's world have worked themselves out. Things are great now, and it would all be lost if I allowed Future Dip to stop Past Dip. Plus, there's some other really cool stuff that Past Dipper has written into this book and it would be a shame if all that hard work he/I did was for nothing.

So before I run out of time, I will explain the secret to time travel. You don't need to get a time travel device. You can create your own if you just know this one basic principle of fourth-dimensional quantum quasar physics. Don't worry, it's very easy to learn.

You just ▮▮▮▮▮▮▮▮▮▮▮▮▮▮▮▮▮▮
▮▮▮▮▮▮▮▮▮▮▮▮▮▮ get a ▮▮
then ▮▮▮▮▮▮▮▮▮▮ ▮▮▮▮▮▮▮▮
▮▮▮▮▮▮▮▮▮▮▮▮▮▮▮▮▮▮▮▮
▮▮▮▮▮▮▮▮▮▮▮▮

▮▮▮▮▮▮▮▮ everything ▮▮▮▮
▮▮▮▮▮▮▮▮ Further ▮▮▮▮
▮▮▮▮▮▮▮▮▮▮ Future
▮▮▮▮▮▮▮▮▮▮▮▮▮▮▮▮▮▮
▮▮▮▮▮▮▮▮ there's ▮▮▮▮
▮▮▮ Past ▮▮▮▮▮▮▮▮
▮▮▮▮▮▮ hard ▮▮▮▮
▮▮▮▮▮▮

▮▮▮▮▮▮▮▮▮▮▮▮ secret
▮▮ You ▮▮▮▮▮▮▮▮▮▮
▮▮▮▮▮▮▮▮▮▮▮▮▮▮▮▮
▮▮▮ 4th ▮▮▮▮▮▮▮
▮▮▮▮ easy ▮▮▮▮

▮▮▮▮▮▮▮▮▮▮ Future
▮▮▮▮▮▮ Further ▮▮▮
time ▮▮▮▮▮▮▮▮
world ▮▮▮▮▮▮▮▮
▮▮▮▮▮▮▮▮▮▮

▮▮▮▮▮▮▮▮▮▮ lost ▮▮
▮▮▮▮ Past ▮▮▮▮▮▮
▮▮▮▮ Past ▮▮▮▮
▮▮▮▮▮▮ all ▮▮
work ▮▮▮▮▮▮▮▮

about

and in

other

all

time

device

dimensional

worry

Further

time

world

Plus

really cool

shame

hard

Simple!

*This chapter edited by Blendin Blandin from the Time Anomaly Removal Crew.

Mabel's NOT HARD, REALLY EASY, Totally Obvious Guide to Time Travel

Step 1—Sit in a chair.

Step 2—look at a clock.

Step 3—You are traveling through time at a rate of 60 seconds per minute.

Codes, Curses, and Other Secret Stuff

So, apparently time travel is a secret that I'm not going to be able to share with you guys. But perhaps my future selves and the Time Anomaly Removal Crew will allow me to write a chapter on some other secret-y biz that won't affect the space-time continuum . . .?

Yes?? We're good? ▽♀♀♀▽▽

Okay, great.

What I should have done is written the previous chapter in code so the Future Spoil Sports couldn't ruin it. But it's too late for that! See, this is why time travel is so useful. Maybe I should go back and . . .

Never mind! Moving on. NOT writing about time travel.

Go to the next page and we'll talk about codes.

History of CODES

∇⇧⇧∇

The ability to translate your message into a secret and confusing language is called cryptography. The more confusing is it, the more powerful it is! Just remember to always use this ancient power for good, and never for evil, for super-evil, or for Lil' Gideon.

NERD ALERT! Mabel here. I'm going to spruce up Dipper's dry page of history with some fun Mabel edits! ◇○◊△△⋂∇

As long as there have been secrets, there have been codes—possibly dating back as far as 500 BC.

(BC? What's that stand for? Boring Codes?!)

Working out how to crack a code is much like solving a puzzle. And since puzzles are fun, cracking codes has long been a form of fun and entertainment for people smart and cool enough to put their brain to the test!

(I like puzzles with cats on them. This chapter needs way more cats!)

Famous Codes:

And now the good stuff! I'm going to teach you how to crack a few codes, but you can't share this information with anyone. Remember, codes work best when they remain a secret! R xzm gifhg blf . . . irtsg? Excuse me, I sneezed!

Caesar Cipher:

This code shifts or rotates the letters of the alphabet to a new meaning, so the letter A becomes the letter B and so on. The alphabet can be shifted up to twenty-six different ways (since there are twenty-six letters in the alphabet). If you rotate the alphabet one place to the right, A becomes B, and the phrase "Dipper is awesome!" becomes "Ejqqfs jt bxftpnf!"

A	B	C	D	E	F	G	H	I	J	K	L	M	N	O	P	Q	R	S	T	U	V	W	X	Y	Z
B	C	D	E	F	G	H	I	J	K	L	M	N	O	P	Q	R	S	T	U	V	W	X	Y	Z	A

Here's how the code works when you shift the letters twelve spots to the right so the letter A becomes the letter M:

A	B	C	D	E	F	G	H	I	J	K	L	M	N	O	P	Q	R	S	T	U	V	W	X	Y	Z
M	N	O	P	Q	R	S	T	U	V	W	X	Y	Z	A	B	C	D	E	F	G	H	I	J	K	L

With this version of the Caesar Cipher, the phrase "Mystery Shack" becomes "Ykefqdk Etmow." Try saying that three times fast! (Or don't . . . you might give yourself a headache.)

Using this Caesar Cipher where A=M, see if you can solve what the following phrase says:

PA KAG FTUZW IQZPK XUWQE YQ?

CODE BREAKER →

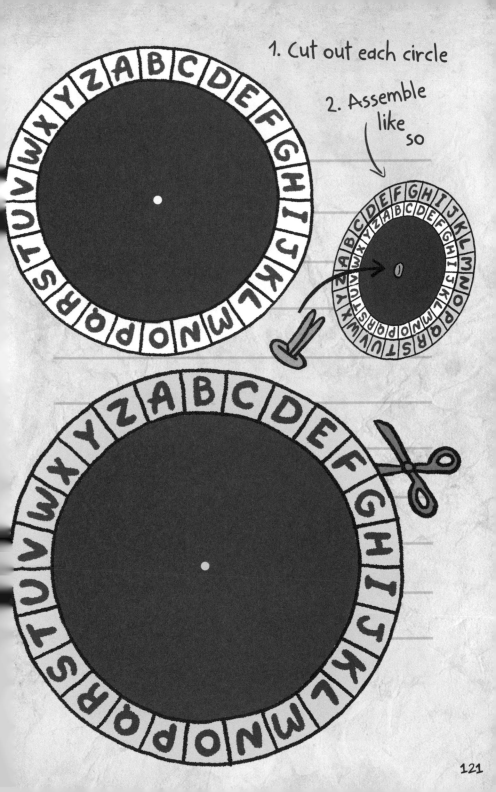

1. Cut out each circle

2. Assemble like so

121

Cracking codes is sooo BORING!

Z Z Z Z Z Z Z

Having a good, complicated, uncrackable code is very important, Mabel!

You know what's uncrackable? My sleepy eyelids after reading this chapter!

BA-ZING!

Atbash Cipher:

This code reverses the alphabet, so A becomes Z, and B becomes Y, and so on.

A	B	C	D	E	F	G	H	I	J	K	L	M	N	O	P	Q	R	S	T	U	V	W	X	Y	Z
Z	Y	X	W	V	U	T	S	R	Q	P	O	N	M	L	K	J	I	H	G	F	E	D	C	B	A

This is a pretty easy code to crack. It only has one possible key, unlike the Caesar cipher's twenty-six possible keys. Try solving this code using the Atbash Cipher:

GIFHG ML LMV

Substitution Cipher:

These codes are really cool because they can code a letter into any symbol, letter, or number you want! For this code, you'll have to get creative and remember where you keep the key so the solution is somewhere nearby at all times!

The first example of a substitution cipher is where we'll replace the letters with numbers:

B	C	D	E	F	G	H	I	J	K	L	M	N	O	P	Q	R	S	T	U	V	W	X	Y	Z
2	3	4	5	6	7	8	9	10	11	12	13	14	15	16	17	18	19	20	21	22	23	24	25	26

With this substitution cipher where A=1 and Z=26 (also known as A1Z26), what does the following phrase say?

18 15 2 2 9 5   9 19   1   10 5 18 11

The coolest thing about substitution ciphers is that you can swap out anything for the letters to customize your own very unique code! Here is a code I just made up:

A	B	C	D	E	F	G	H	I	J	K	L	M	N	O	P	Q	R	S	T	U	V	W	X	Y	Z
9	R	#	<	W	Q	2	{	7	X	P	!	V	*	4	J	D	:	Z	6	E	3	I	%	8	C

Wow! What a confusing and random code! Without this key, it would take forever and be extremely frustrating to crack this code. Because it is so random, be sure not to lose the key or your secrets may be lost even from you! There's no easy way to remember this code like the previous code A1Z26! Try decoding the following phrase using the code key I just created:

```
6{7Z   7Z   I98   V4:W   QE*
  6{9*    247*2   4E6Z7<W
```

Morse Code:

Morse Code, named after inventor and giant-beard-haver Samuel Morse, is another famous code that can be used in a variety of ways. The code is made up of dots and dashes (or "dits" and "dahs" if saying them out loud) that represent different letters. Some radios or walkie-talkies can send signals in beeps or tones that you control. You can send this code with audio by making a quick "dit" with the tone for a dot, or a longer "dah" for a dash. You can also send this code visually by turning a flashlight on and off in similar intervals. This is fun and also confuses the heck out of fireflies.

All this code-cracking is making me dizzy. . . .

I think I'm gonna rest my eyes . . .

for . . .

just a moment. . . .

Well, well, well. Ole Pine Tree really *is* adorable, isn't he? Watching this sentient amalgamation of skin and plasma try to write a decent book *is* like watching a pancake try to teach a class on astrophysics! The only thing Dipper is an "expert" on is how to be in denial about the looming destruction that crawls closer toward humanity with every rotation of their planet around this underwhelming star! His simpleminded codes and supernatural tips won't help him when the rise of my nightmare realm brings forth a . . . well, I'm getting ahead of myself. Let's just say it's gonna be a real party!

Mabel, on the other hand—her, I like. "Fun" is just another way of saying CHAOS, and I'm the master of that! Here's a list of some REALLY fun things:

- Pulling teeth out of a deer's mouth
- Asking "why" until someone runs out of answers and starts sobbing uncontrollably
- Bending your fingers backwards as far as you can
- Eating childhood memories
- Making time stop forever
- Transforming into whatever form people fear most
- Silly straws! They crack me up! They're so silly!

The conspiracies in this book are cute, sure, but they're just the tip of the triangle, you dig? You want to know about some REAL conspiracies? Can you handle some REAL knowledge?

- The moon landing was faked to hide the truth that the moon doesn't exist. It's a two-dimensional disk hiding alien space surveillance.
- Chairs have feelings and you cause them pain whenever you sit on one.
- Western democracy is a sham propped up by an elite cabal of the superrich. They have a really great rec room. I play ping-pong there sometimes!
- Global warming will eventually release something frozen in a glacier that's almost as powerful as me!
- Remember that thing your parents told you? The thing they said was really important, and would make you feel safe and secure and help you sleep at night? They were lying. Pleasant dreams!

Anyway, it's been fun tap-dancing on your heads, but I've got places to be and alternate realities to tamper with! You humans are such tiny-minded folk—you can't see the ultraviolet patterns on flowers, understand the motion of the stars, or hear the thoughts of animals. Heck . . . I bet you can't even figure out the code I've hidden throughout this book!

I'll be back, but remember . . .

NOSTRADAMUS WAS A HACK! MORALITY IS A MENTAL CAGE DESIGNED BY THE WEAK! HOW'S ANNIE?! BYYEEEEEEEEEE!!!!!!!

Oh man, sorry about that last page, everyone. When I woke up I tried erasing it, but it didn't work. It doesn't look like it's written in pencil, ink, or any other substance I know of. I then tried ripping it out, but every time I tried, I started to fall asleep again. Spooky! I'm not sure what Bill Cipher is up to, but I'd just avoid reading that previous page if you haven't already.

Create Your Own Code

Secrecy is more important now than ever before! If Bill is snooping around, you're going to want to keep your messages out of his hands at all costs. Fill out the key below to create your own code! You can use letters, numbers, symbols, or even little drawings to represent a letter! Eat it, Bill! (Don't forget to name your code!)

The _____ Code, invented by Cryptographer

_____

A	B	C	D	E	F	G	H	I	J	K	L	M	N	O	P	Q	R	S	T	U	V	W	X	Y

Using your brand-new code, write a few coded messages and have a friend solve them.

Coded Message: _____

_____

Decoded: _____

_____

Coded Message:

_____

_____

Decoded: _____

_____

_____

Now try making a different code! _____

B	C	D	E	F	G	H	I	J	K	L	M	N	O	P	Q	R	S	T	U	V	W	X	Y	Z

_____

The _____ Code

Coded Message: _____

_____

Decoded: _____

_____

_____

Coded Message: _____

_____

_____

Decoded: _____

_____

_____

Mabel's Craft Corner— SPOOKY BREWS!

Workin' up a supernatural thirst from all that code-cracking? How about we quench that dryness with some Spooky Brews! Dipper's journal explains how to make a lot of cursed and dangerous potions, but I've found that most of them can be transformed into pleasing party punches with the removal of a few key ingredients!

Drink of the Dead

Ingredients:
- Ice • Citrus-flavored soda • large spoonful of lime sherbet
- A splash of lime juice • The blood of your enemies

Mix all the ingredients into a glass, cup, or mug for a potent Spooky Brew! To make a fun and tasty drink that's non-evil, don't add "the blood of your enemies."

Ghoul's Spittoon

Ingredients:
- Can of frozen berry juice • Water
- lemonade • A handful of goblin hair

First mix the frozen concentrate and a can full of water into a pitcher to make the berry juice. Then pour that juice into an ice cube tray. When your berry juice ice cubes are frozen, place them in a glass and pour in your lemonade and goblin hair! (You can replace the goblin hair with sprigs of mint for a tastier drink.)

Code Crackin'

Oh, no! I wrote this supersecret message in code so Mabel couldn't read it, but after drinking some of Mabel's Spooky Brews, I can't remember the code key! Did I use the Atbash Cipher? The A1Z26 Substitution Cipher? Wait, it looks like there's a little Morse Code in there as well . . . I must have mixed all three codes to make a super code!

Can you help me decode my supersecret message?

GL 7520 YZXP ZG 1312512, XZMWB, 1144 TIVMWZ

6 15 18 20 8 5 9 18 — •• –••– –•– •–•• • •– — — — •– –•–• ––•–, R'N

TLRMT 20 15 16 21 20 •–•–•–•–– –••• •• — –•••–••–– ••– 9 14

20 8 5 9 18 HLXPH!

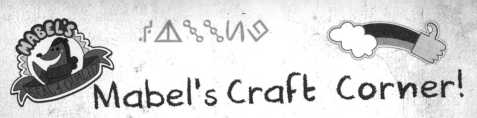

Mabel's Craft Corner!

Time to craft your own language. Ha! Wordplay! But, really, coming up with your own language isn't that hard. Take pig latin, for instance. Totally made up by some kid in, I'm guessing, latin America. It has two simple rules: Take all the consonants at the start of a word, move them to the end, and add "-ay." For words that start with a vowel, just add "-yay." Yay! Sound like fun?

ENGLISH	PIG LATIN
Mabel	Able-may
Cute	Ute-cay
Braces	Aces-bray
Eggs	Eggs-yay

See! Simple. I've made up my own personal language that I call Waddles latin. Can you figure out the pattern?

ENGLISH	WADDLES LATIN
Mabel	Able-maddles
Cute	Ute-caddles
Braces	Aces-braddles
Eggs	Eggs-waddles

Just move the consonants to the end and add "-addles." For words that start with a vowel, just add "-waddles". Everything's better with Waddles!!

Fun-Masters are so busy making dreams come true and raising various roofs that we don't have time for long phrases. That's why we shorten 'em up into acronyms! Everyone knows these common ones:

ᐁᔑᕀᔑᐃᐳᕀᑎᐟ

"BFF"	Best Friends Forever
"BRB"	Be Right Back
"IMHO"	In My Humble Opinion
"lol"	laugh Out loud
"SWAK"	Sealed With A Kiss

Here are some of my own Mabel Brand Acronyms!

"BBFFAEAE"	Best Best Friends Forever And Ever And Ever
"WWWD"	What Would Waddles Do?
"IMAO"	In My AWESOME Opinion
"YUASCC"	Why You Ackin' So Cray Cray?
"TC4ANS"	This Calls For A New Sweater

ROTFlUIRDTSAOTDAOACAOABAATSAOTAWIBTQOTKAATUAM

Rolling On The Floor laughing Until I Roll Down The Stairs And Out The Door And Off A Cliff And Onto A Boat And Across The Sea And Over To Australia Where I Become The Queen Of The Koalas And Aid Their Uprising Against Mankind. (Only use this one under certain very specific circumstances.)

QUEEN OF KOALAS

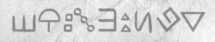

Another kind of language is the language of fashion! Each sweater I wear has a symbol! Can you figure out what each one is?

It's Not POLITE to Curse

It's been said that words can hurt as much as weapons. That's especially true if those words are in the form of a mystical curse. It might be tempting to open your paranormal journal to a random page and yell some crazy sounding junk to get your sister to stop singing boy band songs. But trust me, it always backfires.

Here are the top five reasons to avoid "getting back" at your sibling with a magical curse:

1) Are you prepared to take care of your new dog-sister?

2) You may think your sibling has bad BO now, but wait till they're a troll.

3) If you banish them to the Netherworld, you'll have to go pick them up for dinner.

4) How are they going to help with chores when they have snakes for fingers?

5) Took away their mouth? Welcome to charades for the rest of your life.

SECRET SOCIETIES
Your Ticket Inside

There's nothing that's much more secret than a secret society. These shadowy organizations are often the key to unraveling some of the deepest mysteries in the world. But how do you know if you've stumbled onto a hidden cabal or just a meeting of sinister TV executives? Ask yourself the following questions:

1) **Members like to wear:** A) business attire. B) casual sportswear. C) heavy wool robes with hoods.

2) **They have their meetings in:** A) the local rec hall. B) a member's living room. C) a torch-lit subterranean stone chamber.

3) **At the start of their meeting, they:** A) read the minutes of the last meeting. B) drink punch and chat. C) join hands and start chanting Latin.

4) **When members see each other in everyday life, they:** A) shake hands and set up a business lunch. B) hug and ask about each other's families. C) avoid eye contact and walk quickly in opposite directions.

5) **The emblem of their club:** A) has a protractor, compass, or other ancient tool-like symbol. B) was designed by a member's 10-year-old daughter. C) has serpents and griffins around a medieval shield that is covered in Celtic runes.

*If you've answered "C" to any of these questions, then you have probably discovered a secret society. You will need to infiltrate the group to figure out what they are up to.

Five Secrets of Highly Successful SECRET SOCIETY Members

Keep these tips in mind when trying to join up:

1) Get your robe tailored. Don't just buy one "off the rack."

2) Be ready for the handshake. Don't assume that once you shake hands, it's over. Who knows what extra added gestures and sounds might make up the official greeting?

3) Practice your Latin. Ninety percent of secret societies use this language in their rituals. You can fake it when everyone's chanting together, but what if the supreme leader comes up to you during a break and says "quid novi"? What then??

4) Keep your opinions to yourself. No subject matter, no matter how small, should tip them that you're an imposter.

5) Know when your cover's been blown. If more than one member starts chanting and walking slowly towards you, run.

SECRET SOCIETIES in Real Life!

Believe it or not, world history is riddled with hidden secretive groups—and some are still active today! And if what I've read in *The Paranoia Code* (my favorite novel ever) is true, some of them may be far stranger than they let on. The symbols are everywhere if you know where to look—on money, in graveyards, on car bumper stickers. . . . You just need to be constantly on the lookout! And if anyone ever catches you exploring—run!

Here are the FACTS about REAL Secret Societies!

1) **NAME:** The Freemasons

   FOUNDER: The ancient stoneworkers of England

   MISSION: Freemasons are the most widely known secret society in the world. It is said that being part of this secretive group will allow its members to be connected to the most powerful people on Earth. Sounds bogus—until you realize that George Washington, Franklin Roosevelt, George Bush, astronaut Buzz Aldrin, and countless other presidents and celebrities were members! They claim their mission is charity and brotherhood, but there was a time when people in America were so suspicious of them that there was a political party actually called the Anti-Mason party. I totally get it—everyone is jealous when they're not let into a club!

   SYMBOLS TODAY: The most common Freemason symbol is a compass and square with a G in the center, which I'm gonna guess stands for "Gee, don't you wish you were a member?" Check cemeteries—these are EVERYWHERE.

2) **NAME:** Skull & Bones

   FOUNDER: A secret society in Yale University, Skull & Bones was supposedly founded as part of a rivalry of school debate teams in

1832. I was in debate class once, and it was nowhere near as creepy as this! Members, or "bonesmen," are chosen every year and must go through super creepy and elaborate hazing rituals, including meeting in a tomb, which might sound cool, except can you imagine being locked in a tomb with a bunch of preppy rich nerds overnight? No thanks!

MISSION: Like most secret societies, their main mission is simply to have a place where they can pat their own backs in private and make everyone jealous. Although, considering that their members have included future U.S. presidents, maybe it's not bad to have a friend on the inside!

SYMBOLS TODAY: Their insignia is a skull and crossbones with the number 322 under it. My guess is that's the number of dollars each member carries in their pocket at all times in case they need to tip their butlers.

3) **NAME:** The Royal Order of the Holy Mackerel

FOUNDER: Next to nothing is known about this society, and I wouldn't believe it existed if my great uncle didn't seem to have so much of their stuff lying around.

MISSION: Judging from the name, I assume it's probably just a fishing club or something. I mean, I like fish as much as the next guy, but making a whole club about it? Seems a little cuckoo.

SYMBOLS TODAY: Just take a look around the Mystery Shack. The stuff is everywhere. Tarps, hanging cloths, lots of weird combinations of Egyptian heads, scimitars, stars, and so on. It's almost as if someone with zero knowledge of history just jammed a bunch of mysterious looking stuff together. Whenever I ask Grunkle Stan about it he always changes the subject. But I'll get to the bottom of it one day!

Hey, guys! I need your help to get Waddles through this secret society's underground chamber and back to safety at the Mystery Shack!

Friendship Club!

You know what's better than a secret club? A FRIENDSHIP CLUB! Candy, Grenda, and I have the best friendship club. To be a member, you have to know all the ins and outs of being a best friend.

CUSTOMIZED HUGS!

What are you saying with your hug? A one-armed hug means, "Oh, hi, hey, what's up, casual acquaintance?" A pat on the back with wide-open eyes is a hug usually reserved for an awkward sibling hug. To show you really mean your friendship, use both arms and add a customized flourish to show you really care: a quick double squeeze, a calming back scratch mid-hug, or a vice-like bear hug are all great customizations!

SPIT SISTERS!

It's like being blood brothers, but for girls. You and your friend each spit into your hands and then shake hands together, sealing your friendship in saliva. Then you immediately wash your hands, 'cause you've got spit all over them. Gross.

SASSY SAYINGS!

Whut up, gurrrl? Why you ackin' so cray cray? Uh-UH! Oh, heck no fo' sho', yo! Use these or make up your own. It doesn't matter if what you're saying actually means anything, as long as it's fun to say!

FRIENDSHIP BRACELETS!

Let the world know who your best friend is by making them a friendship bracelet!

THE MYSTERY BLOT

You guys! I turned to this page to write about the most secret secret in Gravity Falls, but then I found this!

What is this symbol?
Where did it come from?
What could it mean . . . ?

The more I look at it, the more I start to see. Like, that part looks an awful lot like Grunkle Stan . . . right?

ᔕᐞᐃᐃᐁ

This could be a message from a supernatural being who is trying to show me something important from the future!

This could be big! I'm going to stare at this for the next few hours and see what kind of things I can find! I'll check back with you guys in a bit.

⸸⋮Ⲷ╫ᑎ ⯅⸸ᒪ⯅ᐯ⯅ᕼᎴᑌᑎ

Okay, you guys. I've been studying the mysterious blot on the previous pages for a full day and I may be losing it a little bit. I've decided to get some outside opinions to help me pinpoint the origins of this blot, which will hopefully help me uncover the mystery behind it!

This thing looks like my memory of the '60s.

◇⯅⯅ℨℨ⅏⯆⅏ᒋ

Aw man, gross! This looks like this one time I spun Thompson around after he ate too many hot dogs and . . . well, let's just say that shape is what splattered on his shoes five minutes later.

I think it looks like friendship! Or intestines!

It looks like a body. But it's changing. Why is it changing?!

▷╫ᑌᑎℨ⅏▽

The MYSTERY BLOT Revealed

Mabel—angelo, here! Dipper's been staring at that blob a few pages back for, like, a billion hours trying to figure out what it means and where it came from. He thinks it's the biggest mystery of all time! But the truth is that I was finger-painting on my latest caticatures (that's a caricature painting where I make everyone look like cats), when I accidentally dripped a big blob of black paint in his book! Naturally, I closed the book to make it look like I wasn't responsible, but that just squished the paint and made it look even weirder. Perfect! Grunkle Stan called the squished painting a "Rorschach test." Apparently, he had to take those tests during his "loony days." I guess whatever you see is supposed to reveal something about you. What do you see?

By the way . . . you can make your own! Find a piece of paper, slather a bunch of paint on only one half, and then fold the paper over in half, making a sort of paint sandwich. When you unfold it, you'll see a mirror image of that paint blob and it'll look neat! See?

Hey everyone, Dipper here. I haven't written in this book for a while, but I think I'm on to something big with that mysterious blobby image that appeared in this very book! My theory is that there was once a librarian who visited Gravity Falls around fifty years ago. While he was in town, he accidentally slipped through a trans-dimensional tear in reality, and he has been trapped in another dimension parallel to this one! Over the years, he has slowly learned how to communicate through multiple dimensions, but his methods are crude and messy—probably because he's developing a whole new type of technology as he goes along!

Man, I am so psyched about this discovery! If I can communicate with him . . . I'll have proved the existence of a multiverse! All I have to do is—oh, it looks like Mabel wrote something on the previous page. I'll give that a quick read, just to see what silliness she's been passing on to you readers. Probably something about how if you drape hair under your nose, it looks like you have a mustache or whatever. Hold on. . . .

Mabel here! Dipper just read my previous page about "the ink blot incident" and he looks . . . well, it's difficult to describe the look on his face. And since we all know a picture is worth like a billion and three words, I'll use my art to express how Dipper looks right now with one of my patented (not really patented) CATICATURES!

Well, that was a waste of three days. Moving on!

DIPPER

Congratulations!

If you've made it this far, read every chapter, taken every quiz, solved every code, and ignored everything Mabel said, then you've completed my crash course in paranormal mysteries! I tip my pine tree hat to you. You are on your way to uncovering the mysteries of the universe, defending the weak, protecting the strange, and making the world a weirder place! I may call upon you one day to join a society that I've been thinking of founding . . . but I have to graduate junior high first! To finally complete your training, and solidify your rank as a Paranormal Expert, read the Oath of the Paranormal Investigator aloud. Repeat after me!

SECRET OATH

I, _____, do solemnly swear to be brave
            (insert name)
in the face of danger but never foolhardy, to trust in the power of magic but be wary of its dark side, and to share the knowledge I gain with all those who believe. EGASSEM SDRAWKCAB! EGASSEM SDRAWKCAB! EGASSEM SDRAWKCAB!

Now black the Oath out with a marker to seal the deal! Cut out the diploma on the following pages, and proudly put it on your wall to let people know that when weirdness attacks, the answer to the question "Who you gonna call?" is YOU!

CONGRATS!!!

Now that you've read all my sections forward and backward (and hopefully upside down) and followed every word of my advice, I declare you to be officially FUN! High five!!!

Remember to always bring the party, never take yourself too seriously, and help the boring people of the world by turning their frowns upside down! Now grab your friends (or make some new ones) and go have a good time!

High Five Here!

Certificate of Mystery

The Bearer of This Document Is a Qualified
Mystery Hunter and a Certified Investigator
of Paranormal Activity.

Dipper Pines

sign here

Dipper Pines

Paranormal Investigator

E PLURIBUS
WEIRDUM

CERTIFICATE OF FUN!!

THIS KID IS CERTIFIED FUN

MABEL MONEH

SIGN HERE

MABEL

YOU'RE A STAR!

Write About the Mysteries in YOUR Town Here

Now that you are among my Mystery Hunting Brethren (and Sister-ren), you must document your own adventures. Write about the mysteries in YOUR town. Who are the strangest people? Where are the creepiest places? Use these pages to record your findings! And if anyone calls you weird, just remember: they're jealous.

o skip ahead o the FUN tuff, jump to age 157!

Add a picture here

Just a few more pages till the FUN

Add a
picture
here

Now that you know about codes, create a new code below and continue writing about your mysteries in code to keep your findings safe.

NO MORE codes!

ZZZᶻ

The _____ Code

	B	C	D	E	F	G	H	I	J	K	L	M	N	O	P	Q	R	S	T	U	V	W	X	Y	Z

Add a picture here ➜

I think mysteries are BORING!

Try writing about something else.
Something exciting! What do you LOVE to do?

Show off your
favorite pastime!

Tell me about your dreams, friend!

Draw your dream!

Tell me your craziest, coolest secrets! No codes required!

Draw an adorable woodland animal!

DOODLE TIME!

Put whatever you want on this page or take my suggestions if you're stuck for ideas.

Draw some sort of monster!

Draw a princess!

Now draw the monster and princess on a date